I grabbed my stuff and ran to the ballet school. I got there early. Well, not exactly *early*. But early for me.

"What's wrong?" Becky asked as soon as I pushed opened the dressing room door.

"Is it something serious, Katie?" Megan said.

"I'm not allowed to—" I started.

Risa came in. "What's going on?" she asked.

"I'm not allowed to take ballet anymore," I blurted out. Then I started to cry. I hardly ever cry. Through my tears, I could see my friends looked freaked out.

Becky put her arm around my shoulders.

"Don't cry," Megan begged. "Just tell us what happened."

I took a deep breath. "My parents don't have the money for lessons," I explained. "They have to save it for baby stuff."

Madame Trikilnova poked her head into the dressing room. "What are you girls doing down here?" she demanded. "Your class has already started."

I didn't want to miss another minute. After all, I only had six more classes to go.

Don't miss any of the books in
this fabulous new series!

#1 Becky at the Barre
#2 Jillian On Her Toes

Coming soon:

#4 Megan's Nutcracker Prince

And look for PONY CAMP —
a great new series from HarperPaperbacks.

Ballet School

Katie's Last Class

Written by

Emily Costello

Illustrated by

Marcy Ramsey

HarperPaperbacks

A Division of HarperCollins*Publishers*

HarperPaperbacks *A Division of* HarperCollins*Publishers*
10 East 53rd Street, New York, N.Y. 10022

Produced by Daniel Weiss Associates, Inc.,
33 West 17th Street, New York, New York 10011.

First printing: September 1994

Printed in the United States of America

HarperPaperbacks and colophon are trademarks of
HarperCollins*Publishers*

10 9 8 7 6 5 4 3 2 1

To Bari Venn, who rode tricycles, played Barbies, and discovered boys with me.

One

Sisters

"Katie?" My little sister, Alison, peeked into my bedroom. "Can I borrow a pair of ballet slippers?"

"What are you going to do with them?" I asked.

"It's a secret," Alison said.

"We'll make you a deal," my best friend, Becky Hill, told Alison. Becky was sitting on my bed. "Katie will give you the slippers. But then you have to promise to leave us alone."

"I promise," Alison said.

Alison is five and a half. She's friends with Becky's little sister, Lena, who is six years old.

Becky is nine, just like me. She has penny-colored hair, fair skin, and freckles. I love Becky's freckles. In the summer the sun makes freckles pop out all over her skin. It's so cool.

My name is Katie Ruiz. If you ask me, I'm not nearly as interesting-looking as Becky. I have brown hair and brown eyes. I have never had even one freckle. Life is unfair.

I pulled a pair of old ballet slippers out of my closet. I didn't mind if Alison played with them. They were too small for me.

"Thanks," Alison said. She took the slippers and disappeared down the hall. Promise or no promise, I knew she would be back soon. My little sister is a true pest.

"What do you think Heather is doing right now?" I asked Becky.

Heather McCabe goes to the same ballet school as Becky and I do. It's called Madame Trikilnova's Classical Ballet School. Becky and I are in the Intermediate I class. Heather is three years older than us. She's one of the best dancers in our school. She takes an advanced class.

Last February Heather tried out for the School of American Ballet's summer session. (Dance people call the School of American Ballet *SAB*.)

SAB is in New York City. Their summer session is a big deal. Not just anyone gets to go. Thousands of kids from all over the country try out for about a hundred spots.

(My friends and I were too young to try out. You have to be at least twelve.)

Heather didn't tell anyone at Madame Trikilnova's that she had tried out. She didn't want anyone to know in case she wasn't picked.

But Heather *was* picked! Everyone at our ballet school was so excited. Imagine how you would feel if someone from your school got a big part in a movie. You'd be happy, right? Well, that's exactly how we felt.

Heather had left for New York City a week earlier. She had never been away from home before and she went to New York alone. Pretty brave, huh?

Becky thought about my question. A dreamy look crossed her face. "Right now, Heather's probably standing in a spotlight," she suggested, "dancing with Nilas Martins." (Nilas Martins dances for the New York City Ballet. He's very handsome.)

"Get real!" I said. "*I* bet she's in class. Some mean ballet teacher is making her do the same step over and over. She's sweating, and getting megablisters."

Becky threw a pillow at me. "Why can't you imagine something nice?"

"Why can't you get your head out of the clouds?" I asked.

As I spoke, Becky mouthed the words I was saying. She often guesses what I'm going to say. That's because we've been best friends practically forever.

Becky drives me crazy sometimes. For example,

she's planning to be a ballerina when she grows up. I mean, I like ballet, too, but I know how hard it is to become a real ballerina. It's a nearly impossible dream. But Becky says that as long as there's the slightest chance, she has to try.

Becky is a dreamer.

My dad says I'm a *realist*. That's a person who faces facts.

"Heather might be sight-seeing," Becky said. "Maybe she's on top of some super-tall building. Or she could be floating around Manhattan in a boat."

See? Becky was doing it again! She was getting all starry-eyed. I had to bring her back to earth.

"Maybe Heather's stuck in the subway," I said.

Becky ignored my comment. "Did you hear that?" she asked.

"What?" I said. But then I heard it. A thud. It had come from Alison's room.

"What are the pests up to now?" I wondered out loud.

Before Becky could reply, Lena and Alison leaped through my door. "Ta da!" they yelled.

"We're ballet dancers," Lena announced.

Alison and Lena don't actually know how to dance ballet. They're too young to take lessons. (You have to be at least seven before you can start at Madame Trikilnova.)

"Get lost, you guys," Becky said. "We're busy."

Becky was getting fed up with Alison and Lena.

I thought they were funny. Or, at least, they *looked* funny.

Lena was wearing a red T-shirt and a grass skirt from Hawaii. Alison had on her bathing suit and a pair of heart-shaped sunglasses. She was wearing my ballet slippers. They were much too big for her.

"Come here, you guys," I said. "I'll show you how to do a real *grand jeté*." (*Grand jeté* means "big leap" in French. All ballet steps have French names. That's because the first ballet school was in France.)

I went and stood against the wall of my room. I ran three steps forward. Then I jumped, stretching my right leg in front of me and my left leg back. My left arm went to the front and my right arm to the side. I landed softly.

"That was pretty!" Becky exclaimed.

"I want to try it," Alison said.

"Me too," Lena agreed.

They ran to the wall.

"Like this?" Alison demanded. She ran, jumped, landed, and fell down.

"No," I said with a laugh. "*Nothing* like that."

"Becky, look at me!" Lena yelled. She ran across the room and threw herself into the air.

6

She landed on top of Alison. The two girls lay on the floor, giggling.

"What's going on up here?" My father stepped into the room. "You girls sound like a herd of elephants."

My dad is a professor at Seattle University. He doesn't teach any classes in the summer, though. Instead he writes long articles only other professors would want to read. About twice a week in the summer he drags me and Alison to the library so he can look things up in books.

"Katie is giving us a ballet lesson," Alison announced.

I winked at Dad.

He smiled back.

My dad is tall. He has green eyes and a bushy beard.

"I hate to interrupt your lesson, Ali," Dad told my sister. "But it's time for Becky and Katie to get ready for their ballet class."

Becky jumped up right away. "I'm ready to go," she announced. "I have my dance bag with me."

"It's too hot for ballet," I said. "Let's go swimming instead."

"Yeah!" Alison yelled.

"Sorry, Ali," my dad said. He gave me a please-don't-cause-trouble look. "We can't go swimming now.

Katie has ballet. Get a move on," he added to me.

"Yeah," Becky said. "Hurry."

I spent ten minutes packing my dance bag. It usually only takes me about thirty seconds. But I was trying to drive Becky crazy. She likes to be extra early to ballet. I would have taken even longer, but Becky started to freak.

"You have until the count of three," Becky told me. "If you aren't ready by then, I'm leaving without you. One . . ."

I pretended to study my feet. "Do you think I should change my shoes?" I asked.

"Two, three!" Becky grabbed my arm and pulled me toward the stairs. "Let's go!"

"Don't forget," I yelled to my dad as Becky dragged me past his office, "I'm going to be late coming home."

Becky and I were going to the airport after ballet class. Our friend Jillian Kormach was flying to New York.

Jillian's parents are divorced. She lives with her mother most of the time. But she was going to visit her dad in New York for the next two weeks.

"No sweat," Dad called back. "We're going to eat dinner late. Your mother has a doctor's appointment after work."

Becky ran out the door in front of me.

I caught up with her on the sidewalk.

"Is your mother sick?" Becky asked. We started walking toward the ballet school.

"No," I said. "I don't know why she's going to the doctor. All I know is that my parents have been acting mysterious for a couple of days."

Becky raised her eyebrows. "What do you mean?"

"This morning my mother was in the bathroom for a very long time," I said. "I thought maybe she was sick. When she came out, I asked her if she was okay. She just smiled and said she was brushing her teeth. For fifteen minutes? I mean—come on!"

Becky shrugged. "That's not a big deal."

"Well, listen to this," I said. "Mom had toast, cereal, *and* an entire grapefruit for breakfast."

"So?" Becky said.

"She usually doesn't eat breakfast at all," I explained.

"Hmm," Becky said.

"My dad asked my mother how she felt," I added. "Guess what she said."

"What?" Becky asked.

"She said, 'I feel like the answer is yes,'" I replied. "What's *that* mean?"

"It means your parents are acting mysterious," Becky said. "Just like last summer."

"I remember," I said. "They acted nutty for a few days. And then they told me I had to go to St. Anthony's."

St. Anthony's is a private Catholic school. I started going there last fall. One of my friends from ballet attends St. Anthony's, too. Her name is Risa Cumberland.

Becky and I were in the same kindergarten, first- and second-grade classes. We were really bummed out when my parents made me switch schools.

Can I tell you a secret? My parents made me change schools because of a test I took. It was an intelligence test. I did really well on it.

My mom and dad were surprised. See, my grades at public school weren't so hot. I didn't work very hard, and the teachers didn't pay much attention to me. At St. Anthony's the classes are smaller, and everyone gets a lot more attention. My grades are much better now, and even though I miss Becky, I like my new school.

"I know!" Becky said. "Your mother probably had the cordless phone in the bathroom. I bet she was talking to someone about putting a pool in your backyard!"

I laughed. Like I said, Becky is a dreamer.

Two

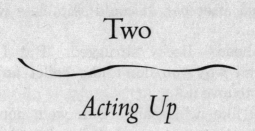

Acting Up

"I have an idea!" I said, grabbing Becky's arm on the way to ballet. The school is about six blocks from my house. Becky and I were almost there.

"What?" she asked.

"Let's skip class," I said.

"And do what?"

"We could sneak into the movie theater," I suggested.

Becky shook her head. "We'd get caught."

"We could rent a video and watch it at your house," I said. "Your mom's at work. And Lena is at my house."

"Sophie is probably at home with her friends," Becky said. Sophie is Becky's older sister. She's thirteen.

"Sophie won't tell on us," I said.

"Listen, I *want* to go to class," Becky told me.

She started marching toward the school.

I trailed after her. "I could skip class without you."

"Go ahead." Becky shrugged. "But I don't understand why you don't like ballet anymore. You used to love it."

"I still like it," I said. "But, well, don't you think going three times a week is too much?"

In the winter we take ballet twice a week. But during the summer we go on Tuesdays, Thursdays, *and* Saturdays.

Our teacher's name is Pat. She's the best. Pat never yells at us when we mess up steps. And the way she lets us call her Pat instead of Ms. Kelly is cool.

The girls in our class call themselves Pat's Pinks. We wear pink leotards and tights to class.

"Three classes a week isn't that much," Becky told me. "During the winter you take three dance classes a week. Two ballet and one modern." (My modern dance class doesn't meet during the summer.)

"Okay," I said. "I'll tell you the truth. I don't want to go to class because of Madame Trikilnova. We never have any fun when she's around. And she's been coming to all of our classes this summer."

Madame Trikilnova owns the ballet school. She's very mean and very strict.

"She's not teaching any classes this summer," Becky said. "Maybe she's bored."

"Then she should go on vacation," I said.

Becky took my hand. "Maybe she won't come to our class today," she said. "Besides, we have to meet Jillian at ballet. Don't you want to go to the airport?"

"Yes," I admitted. I let Becky pull me along.

"We're here," Becky yelled as we walked into the dressing room. "Finally."

"Hi," Megan Isozaki said. She was sitting on a bench in front of the lockers. Jillian was standing over Megan, French-braiding her hair. She gave us a little wave.

Megan is tiny. She's Japanese-American. She's good at cheering people up when something bad happens.

Jillian has terrific dark eyes and long eyelashes. Jillian acts more grown-up than the rest of us. That's probably because she moved here from New York City. Jillian is African-American.

"Hmmrh," Risa mumbled in greeting. She was brushing her hair up into a bushy ponytail on top of her head. A ponytail holder was in her mouth.

Risa's mother makes her take ballet. Mrs.

Cumberland thinks dance classes will give Risa grace. So far it hasn't worked.

"Katie, what are you doing here so early?" Nikki Norg asked. "Class doesn't start for ten minutes."

Nikki was teasing me. I'm kind of famous for being late. "I came with Becky," I told her.

"That explains it," Nikki said. Becky is just as famous for being early.

Nikki's mother makes her take ballet, too. Mrs. Norg also makes Nikki try out for plays and movies and commercials. She wants Nikki to be a star. She doesn't care that Nikki isn't really into performing. Mrs. Norg isn't a total meanie, though. She let Nikki get her ears pierced. (None of my other friends are allowed. Neither am I.) That day Nikki was wearing whale earrings.

"See you guys upstairs," Becky said.

Amazing. I hadn't even opened my dance bag yet. But Becky was already dressed. She always does about a million stretches in the studio while the rest of us hang out in the dressing room.

"Are you excited about going to New York?" Megan asked Jillian.

"Totally," Jillian said. "I can't wait to see my dad! I haven't seen him since March."

14

Poor Jillian. I would hate it if my dad lived far away.

"That must be awful," I said, stepping into my tights.

"It's not that bad," Jillian said. "We talk on the phone once a week. Guess what? Dad moved out of our old apartment."

"That's terrible!" Megan exclaimed.

"No, it's not," Jillian said. "It's terrific! Our old apartment was in Brooklyn. It was nice but not very exciting. The new apartment is in Manhattan, and it's on the twenty-fourth floor! Dad says it has a terrific view. He also said there's a movie theater right down the street. And tons of great restaurants. I can't wait to get there."

"I wish I could go," Nikki said.

"That would be so much fun," Risa added.

Megan nodded.

"I can't believe you're going to be gone for two weeks," I said. "We'll miss you."

When Jillian first moved here, I didn't like her. I thought she was a big show-off. She bragged about New York all the time. Now that she knows us better, she doesn't show off as much. I like her a lot more. (Besides, now that we're friends, I can tell her to shut up if she's bugging me.)

"I hope nothing exciting happens while I'm gone," Jillian said.

"Don't worry," Nikki said. "Nothing exciting ever happens in Glory."

Glory, Washington, is our hometown. Some of my friends, like Nikki, think it's boring. *I* love it. The town is right in the mountains, the ocean is nearby, and Seattle is not too far away. What more could you want?

I finished getting dressed and sat down next to Megan.

Giselle, the ballet school cat, jumped onto my lap. I love cats. Giselle is beautiful. She has orange and white tiger stripes. I kissed the top of her head.

"Aren't you going to put your hair up?" Megan asked.

I groaned. I absolutely, positively hate dancing with my hair smooshed up in a bun. It's no fun. In my modern dance class we're allowed to wear our hair in a ponytail. Sometimes my teacher even lets us wear it down. That feels terrific. I love the way my hair whips around when we do turns.

"No," I said, making up my mind. "I want to wear it down."

My friends looked shocked.

"You *have* to put your hair up," Jillian told me. "It's a rule."

"Ballet has too many rules," I said.

Risa and Jillian exchanged looks. They think I make too many ballet-is-too-traditional speeches. Becky would have agreed with them.

"But there's a reason we have to wear our hair up," Megan argued. "It's so Pat can see our necks and shoulders."

"And so our hair doesn't swing in our faces," Risa added.

"I don't care," I said.

"Katie should be allowed to wear her hair down if she wants to," Nikki said.

Risa smiled. "You'd better not listen to Nikki," she warned me. "Madame Trikilnova doesn't like *her* hair either."

About two months earlier, Nikki had gotten her waist-length hair cut super short. Nikki loves her short hair, but Madame Trikilnova ordered her to grow it out. She said ballerinas were supposed to have long hair.

"I dance fine with short hair," Nikki said. Risa had only been teasing, but Nikki sounded huffy.

"And I'll dance better with my hair down," I said.

Risa shook her head. "No, you won't."

"Why not?" I asked.

"Pat will never let you dance that way," Risa said.

17

"Pat will let me do what I want," I argued.

"Let's go upstairs and find out," Megan said. "Class is going to start any minute."

Jillian and Megan and Nikki and Risa and I trooped out into the hall. We were starting up the stairs when I heard a loud voice behind us.

"Miss Ruiz!"

I spun around. Madame Trikilnova was standing at the bottom of the stairs. Her hair was in a tidy bun. It always is. She pulls it so tight, it will probably fall right out of her head one day.

"Yes, Madame Trikilnova?" I asked sweetly.

"It's silly to go to class if you aren't prepared to dance," she said. "Go put up your hair. The rest of you, please get upstairs. Your class is about to begin."

My friends started to climb the stairs.

Madame Trikilnova headed down the hall to her office.

I stomped back into the dressing room and opened my locker with a bang. Who did Madame Trikilnova think she was, anyway? She wasn't my teacher. I didn't want her telling me what to do.

18

Three

Small-Town Girl

"Hi, Katie," Pat said as I came into the studio.

Al, the piano player, winked at me.

I stuck my tongue out at him. (I wasn't mad at Al. I was still feeling grumpy about Madame Trikilnova.)

My mother says Al is a *character*. He has a messy mop of brown hair. He rides his bicycle to class. One of his pants legs is always taped down so it won't get caught in the gears. He keeps his bicycle helmet on top of the piano.

"Everyone is here," Pat called out. "Let's start."

We all scrambled for spots at the barre. (A barre is a wooden handrail. You hold on to it while you do exercises.)

I ended up standing between Megan and Nikki. Becky was standing up front, like she always does.

There were nine kids in our summer class. You already know about Becky, Risa, Jillian, Megan, Nikki, and me. There were also John Stein, Charlotte Stype, and Lynn Frazier.

Three of the kids who were in our class during the winter were away. Kim Woyczek was visiting her grandmother in Ohio. The Stellar twins, Philip and Dean, were going to football camp instead of taking dance. Dean really missed ballet. (And I was pretty sure he missed a certain someone in our class. More about that later.)

Pat showed us the exercise she wanted us to do. Al began to play.

We started a series of half knee-bends. (In ballet language half knee-bends are called *demi-pliés*.) We did four *demi-pliés* with our left hands on the barre. Then we rose up onto the balls of our feet (that's called a *relevé*) and turned till we faced the opposite side. We did four more *demi-pliés* with our right hands on the barre.

Did you know that ballet classes have a set order? They do. It goes like this:

Barre exercises come first. They don't change much from class to class.

After your muscles are warmed up from the barre, you move into the center of the studio. In the center you do many of the exercises over again—but you don't have anything to hold on to. That's why you need good balance to do the center exercises.

Toward the end of the class, you get to do traveling steps, jumps, and combinations. A traveling step is one that moves you across the floor to the front, back, or side. A combination is a few steps put together into a minidance.

I think the end of class is more fun than the beginning. So does Becky. But not everyone agrees. Megan likes barre best. Combinations make her nervous.

"Why do we always start with *pliés*?" I asked Nikki. "It drives me crazy."

"Me too," Nikki whispered back. Her earrings flashed as she did another *demi-plié*. "I bet we do *tendus* next."

"Okay," Pat said just then. "Next I want you to *tendu* to the front, two, three . . ."

Nikki and I groaned.

"We've done about a thousand *tendus* this summer," I complained.

"More like a million," Nikki whispered.

I learned how to do *tendus* in my very first ballet class. To do a *tendu* to the front, you start in first, third, or fifth position and extend your foot to fourth position. Then you bring it back again.

Pat is always dreaming up a new *tendu* exercise. They're all boring. *Tendus* are like oatmeal. It doesn't matter what kind of fancy fruit you slice on top, underneath is a blop of blah mush.

"That's lovely, Becky," Pat said. She was walking around the room, watching each of us do our *tendus*. "Nikki, be careful not to bend your knees."

Pat came and stood next to me.

"I'm sick of *tendus*," I told her. "Please teach us something new."

"Even important ballerinas have to practice their *tendus*," Pat told me. "You can learn a lot from trying to do them perfectly. I want you to work on your turnout, Katie."

Groan. Pat is always picking on my turnout.

Turnout is a big thing in ballet. It means turning your legs out to the side from the hip. Lots of people have natural turnout. I'm not one of those people.

I was sick of working on my turnout.

Pat moved on and stood where she could watch Megan.

Nikki turned around and grinned at me. "Nice try."

"Do me a favor," I told her. "Wake me up if I fall asleep."

Nikki giggled.

"Have you seen Chris Adabo lately?" I whispered.

Chris Adabo is this super-cute boy. He's twelve and he takes an advanced class at the ballet school. He has great green eyes.

"No," Nikki said. "I miss him."

Just then Madame Trikilnova came into the studio.

I sighed. I was still angry at Madame Trikilnova for making me put my hair up. Why did she have to interrupt my class, too?

Madame Trikilnova and Pat started talking in quiet voices. After we finished our *tendus*, there was nothing to do except stand around and wait for Pat. Still, the class remained super quiet. Everyone was afraid to make noise since Madame Trikilnova was there. I could hardly stand it. Things were really getting boring.

"Can we take a break?" I called out.

Pat looked up. "No," she said. She turned away from Madame long enough to show us an exercise with *dégagés*."

Dégagés are a lot like *tendus*, except that after you extend your foot you get to lift it off the ground.

Zzzz.

The grown-ups spoke quietly for a few more seconds. Then Madame Trikilnova handed Pat a pink envelope.

Pat put the envelope on top of the piano. Then she walked back to her place in the front of the studio and gave the class her full attention. She did the last few *dégagés* with us. Then she said, "Let's move on to some *ronds de jambe à terre*."

Ronds de jambe means "rounds of the leg." *A terre* is French for "on the ground." You can also do the exercise *en l'air*. That means "in the air." When I was little, I called *ronds de jambe* "half-circles," because when you do the exercise, you draw half-circles with your toe.

Pat started to count. We started the exercise. But Madame Trikilnova didn't leave. She stood next to the door and watched us.

The other kids were trying extra hard to dance well. They always do when Madame Trikilnova watches our class.

Madame Trikilnova is a big deal at our school. Becky *loves* her. Everyone wants to impress her. Well, everyone except for me.

I do not like Madame Trikilnova. And not just because she told me to put my hair up. She also yelled at me a few times for being late. Plus, she was mean to Nikki about her haircut. She yelled at Becky's mom at Becky's recital last year. She tried to kick Jillian out of the ballet school. I'm telling you, the woman is a first-class grump.

"Maybe we'll see Chris after class," I whispered to Nikki.

"Shh!" Nikki hissed.

"What's your problem?" I asked.

Nikki didn't answer.

"Chicken," I whispered.

Madame Trikilnova clapped her hands.

Al stopped playing.

"Miss Ruiz," Madame Trikilnova said. "Come here."

I walked to the front of the studio. Everyone was staring at me. When I got close to her, Madame Trikilnova put on her glasses. (She wears them on a chain around her neck.) She studied my face for a long time.

I stared back at her.

"Miss Ruiz," Madame Trikilnova said. She was talking loudly enough for everyone to hear. "You have a bad attitude. You need to work harder."

I didn't say anything.

Madame Trikilnova glared at me. I think she was waiting for me to agree. But I still didn't say anything.

Madame Trikilnova turned and stormed out the door.

I walked back to my place at the barre.

Charlotte Stype gave me an evil smile.

My friends looked horrified. Especially Becky.

I rolled my eyes. I wanted everyone to know I didn't care what Madame Trikilnova said.

Pat continued the class. We finished the barre, did center work, and learned a quick combination. I wasn't paying much attention in class, though. I was thinking about how Madame Trikilnova had spoiled my entire summer of ballet. I didn't like it one bit.

Class ended, and everyone clapped. (It's a tradition to clap for your teacher and piano player at the end of a ballet class.)

Pat picked up the envelope on the piano. She opened it and pulled out the letter inside. As Pat read, a big frown formed on her face.

"What's wrong?" I asked.

"Oh, this letter . . ." Pat said.

"Who's it from?" I asked.

"Heather McCabe," Pat replied.

"What's wrong with Heather?" came a voice.

I turned around. Most of the class had gathered behind Pat and me. Since Heather had been accepted at the School of American Ballet, she had become famous at Madame Trikilnova's. A letter from her was big news.

"Heather is homesick," Pat reported. "She wants to drop out of SAB and come back to Glory."

"No way," Becky said.

"Heather wrote to Madame Trikilnova and told her how unhappy she was," Pat explained. "I spent a summer at SAB when I was Heather's age. That's why Madame Trikilnova wants me to answer the letter. I hope I can think of something encouraging to say."

"Tell Heather she's being a baby," Charlotte suggested. "She isn't in New York to have fun. She's there to dance."

I felt like stomping on Charlotte's toes.

Charlotte has always been stuck-up. But recently she's gotten even worse. She's been picking on Becky.

See, Charlotte has always been the best dancer in Pat's class. But for the last few months Becky's dancing has gotten better and better. The better Becky dances, the meaner Charlotte is to her. I think Charlotte is worried that Becky will be the best Pat's Pink soon.

"I feel sorry for Heather," Lynn Frazier said. "How can she dance well if she's unhappy?"

Lynn is Charlotte's best friend. But I like her anyway. Lynn laughs a lot, and she's friendly to everyone.

"I'm sure Heather isn't dancing her best," Pat told Lynn.

"So you think she should come home?" Becky asked. She sounded disappointed.

"I didn't say that," Pat replied. "I just wish we could think of a way to cheer her up."

"How about a way to make her *grow* up instead?" Charlotte said. She headed for the studio door, looking disgusted.

Lynn ran after her.

"Um, you guys?" Jillian said to me and Becky and Megan. "We should get ready. I promised my mother we'd meet her right after class. She doesn't want us to be rushed at the airport."

Pat snapped her fingers. "Jillian," she said. "I forgot you were on your way to New York. You should call Heather when you get there. Leave her a message at SAB. Will your dad help you find the number?"

Jillian turned her dark eyes to the floor. "I already have the number," she told Pat. "But what would I say? Heather doesn't even know who I am."

"Remind her that she danced for our class a few months ago," Pat suggested. "Remember when she was here?"

Jillian nodded.

"I'm sure Heather will remember you," Pat went on. "And talking to someone from Glory might help her with her homesickness."

29

"Okay, I'll call," Jillian agreed. Then she turned to us. "Come on. Let's go."

Becky, Megan, Risa, Nikki, Jillian, and I hurried downstairs, changed into our street clothes, and went outside.

Jillian's mother—her name is Ms. Bell—was sitting in her car at the curb. She waved when she saw us.

Jillian turned to Nikki and Risa. They weren't coming to the airport with the rest of us. There wasn't room for everyone in Ms. Bell's car.

"See you guys," Jillian said.

"Bye," Nikki said.

"Have fun in New York," Risa added.

"I'm taking Megan's address with me," Jillian said. "I'll send all of you a letter at her house."

"Great," Risa said.

The three of them shared a quick hug. Then Jillian, Becky, Megan, and I climbed into the car.

Ms. Bell beeped the horn a few times as she pulled away from the curb.

"I'd love to go to New York," Megan said once we were on the highway. "I wonder why Heather doesn't like it there."

"New York can be scary," Jillian said. "The city is exciting, but sometimes it seems *so* big. I can't imagine being there alone, without knowing anybody."

"Heather needs a friend," I said.

"And a tour guide," Becky put in.

Jillian grinned. "Maybe I can be both!"

"Are you going to take some ballet classes in New York?" Becky asked Jillian.

"If I can," Jillian said. "It's going to be time to try out for *The Nutcracker* soon. I want to be Clara this year."

"Me too," Becky agreed.

The Nutcracker is a Christmas ballet. Clara is one of the most important characters in it. She's usually played by a girl our age. All of Pat's Pinks wanted to be Clara. Charlotte was positive she was going to get the part.

"I think that's why Madame Trikilnova has been coming to our class so much this summer," Megan said. "She's starting to look for someone to play Clara."

I can forget getting the part, I told myself. Madame Trikilnova would never let *me* be Clara.

Four

Major News

The next day, my father dragged me and Alison to the library at the University of Seattle. Alison and I spent all day curled up in comfy chairs, reading. I read all of *Winnie-the-Pooh* to Alison. By the time we got to the end of the book, my voice was exhausted.

Dad got a lot of work done. That made him happy. He bought us Popsicles after lunch. Later on he whistled while he cooked dinner.

When dinner was ready, we all sat down and joined hands.

"Alison," Dad said. "Why don't you say grace?"

"Good bread," Alison said. "Good meat, good God, let's eat."

Dad likes us to take grace seriously. But he laughed. He really *was* in a good mood.

"How's ballet going?" Mom asked me. She held her hand out for my plate.

I gave my plate to her. I watched her fill it with brown rice and steamed vegetables.

"Ballet has been the worst lately," I said. "Madame Trikilnova keeps coming to our class, and ruining it. I think she's already trying to decide who will make the best Clara. Can you believe her? I mean, *Nutcracker* tryouts aren't until November."

Mom passed my plate to Dad, who put a piece of fish on it.

"Aren't you excited?" Dad asked. "You might get to be Clara this year."

"No I won't," I said.

"How do you know?" Mom asked.

I could tell she was getting ready to make a speech. You can do anything you set your mind to, she'd tell me. I tried to figure out how to explain. I couldn't say Madame Trikilnova hated me. My parents would never understand. They might even think it was *my* fault. But before I could say anything, something happened that made my family forget all about *The Nutcracker*.

"Marian," my dad said, "I made a piece of fish for you." He leaned over and scooped the fish onto Mom's plate. (Marian is Mom's first name.)

For a second Mom looked surprised. "Thanks," she said slowly. Then she did something I had never seen her do before—she took a bite of fish.

My parents are vegetarians. That means they don't eat meat, chicken, or fish. But they still cook it for me and Alison. They want us to make our own choices about what we eat when we get older.

"Mom!" I yelled. "What are you doing?"

"Stop!" Alison put in. "It's fish!"

My parents laughed.

"I think we'd better tell them," Mom said to Dad.

"Go ahead."

Mom took one of my hands and one of Alison's.

I knew something big was coming.

"You two are going to have a new little brother or sister."

My jaw dropped. Wow! No wonder my parents had been acting mysteriously lately! I suddenly understood why Mom had been going to the doctor when she wasn't sick.

"Neat-o!" Alison yelled, bouncing up and down in her seat.

"This is cool," I told my parents. "Having a baby in the family will be so much fun."

"It'll also be a lot of *work*," Dad said. "I remember when you guys were babies. You were really a handful."

"That's because you and Mom didn't have anyone to help you," I said. "But now you have me!"

"And me," Alison said.

Dad smiled at us. "Are you two going to help us change diapers?" he asked.

"No diapers," I decided. "But I can do lots of other stuff. I can teach the baby how to walk and talk and dance. It's going to be great."

I imagined myself pushing the baby on a swing. Or saving the baby from a bully. The baby's first words would probably be "I love Katie." Maybe Mom would have twins! Then I could do twice as many helpful things.

"What's the baby's name?" Alison asked.

Dad laughed. "We haven't decided yet," he said. "We don't even know if the baby will be a boy or a girl."

"I want to help pick out a name," Alison said. "I know lots of good ones."

I almost spit out my milk. Good names? Alison's favorite doll is named Harold! And it's supposed to be a *girl*.

"That's a wonderful idea," Mom said.

Dad nodded.

"This is what we'll do," Mom announced. "Alison can pick out a boy's name for the baby. And you can pick out a girl's name, Katie."

"Mom," I said. "Are you *sure*? This will be the baby's name forever." I was hoping she would change her mind. I didn't want to go through life with a little brother named Beatrice.

Mom winked at me. "I'm positive," she said. "I trust you two to do a good job."

Five

The Voice of Experience

"My mother is going to have a baby!" I announced.

"Wow!" Becky said.

Megan's eyes opened wider.

"Cool!" Nikki said.

It was a little later that same evening. I was having a slumber party. Becky, Megan, and Nikki had already arrived. We were sitting on my front porch, waiting for Risa.

"You're so lucky," Megan told me. "I would love to have a little brother or sister. I'm tired of being the baby in my family."

"One little brother is enough for me," Nikki said. "But a little *sister* would be neat. That would make it two girls against one boy in my family. Georgie would never get his way again." (Georgie is Nikki's little brother.)

Risa came up my walk. "What's up?" she asked

as she put her sleeping bag and overnight bag down on the porch.

"Katie's mother is going to have a baby," Becky said.

"That's too bad," Risa said. She sat down on the porch swing.

"I'm really happy about it," I told her.

"I remember when I was happy that Colette was going to have Sara," Risa said.

Risa's parents are divorced. Her dad married Colette about three years ago. That makes Colette Risa's stepmother. Sara is Colette and Mr. Cumberland's daughter.

Risa shook her head and laughed. "I can't believe I was ever excited about a new baby. I was so stupid!"

I didn't like the way Risa was acting. I was getting a funny feeling in my stomach.

"What do you mean?" I asked. "Don't you like Sara anymore?"

Risa didn't answer my question. "Things didn't get really bad until after Sara came home from the hospital," she said. "Dad and Colette didn't get any sleep for months."

"Why not?" Becky asked.

"Sara woke up in the middle of the night every night," Risa explained. "She'd scream until everyone was awake."

"What was wrong with her?" Nikki asked.

Risa laughed. "Nothing! She was just hungry. Babies like to eat in the middle of the night."

"That's weird," Megan said.

"It's *awful*," Risa said. "After staying up with the baby half the night, Dad didn't have the energy to do anything with me. Everything was Sara, Sara, Sara all the time."

"Sara's pretty big now," I said. "I bet things are getting a lot better."

"Not really," Risa told me. "Sara's fourteen months old. She's in this grabby stage. She touches everything with her slobbery fingers. All my stuff gets sticky."

"Ugh," Nikki said.

"I'm just glad I don't have to live with Sara all the time," Risa went on. "I only have to deal with her when I visit my dad."

Oh, great. My parents weren't divorced. *I* was going to have to live with the new baby *all* the time.

"Wait a second!" I said to Risa. "How come you never complain about Sara at school? You're just saying this stuff to get me worried, aren't you?"

Risa looked serious. "Why would I do that?" she asked. "I don't talk about Sara because I don't like to *think* about her."

There was a long pause. That funny feeling in

my stomach got much bigger. I was beginning to wish we could talk about something else.

Megan glanced around the circle. "I don't mean to change the subject—" she started.

"That's okay," I said quickly. "Go ahead."

"I saw Jillian's mother at the coffee shop," Megan announced. "She talked to Jillian on the phone this afternoon. Guess what? Jillian called Heather! Heather told Jillian that she's really homesick."

"I feel sorry for Heather," Becky said. "But I still don't want her to come home."

"Don't worry," Megan said. "Mr. Kormach offered to let Heather move in with him and Jillian until SAB's summer session ends. Heather's parents already said it was okay."

"You're kidding!" Risa exclaimed.

"Mr. Kormach must be nice," Becky said.

Nikki nodded. "I thought apartments in New York were tiny."

"Mr. Kormach's must be big enough," Megan said. "Remember how Jillian said her dad moved to Manhattan?"

We all nodded.

"Well, his new apartment is in the same neighborhood as SAB," Megan told us. "It's super convenient for Heather."

"Why does Heather want to live with the Kormachs?" Nikki wondered. "It's not like she's friends with Jillian."

"They know a lot of the same people," Megan pointed out.

"And it's probably nicer than living in a dormitory," I added.

"I bet the food is better, too," Risa said.

"I don't care why," Becky said. "I'm just glad Heather isn't quitting SAB."

"Hi, everybody," a small voice said. "Did Katie tell you?"

My friends and I turned around. Alison was standing in the doorway.

"Do you mean about the baby?" Becky asked.

Alison nodded. "I'm hoping for a boy."

Becky raised her eyebrows. "You want a brother?"

"Yes," Alison said. "If the baby's a boy, I get to pick his name. I already decided. My little brother is going to be called Christopher Robin Ruiz!" (Remember I told you that I read Alison *Winnie-the-Pooh*?)

My friends laughed. I shook my head.

Alison looked pleased with herself. She likes to make people laugh. She ran back into the house.

"My parents are making a serious mistake," I said. "How can they let Alison pick out the baby's name?"

"I don't think she's doing a bad job," Nikki said.

41

"At least she doesn't want to name the baby Eeyore."

"Or Piglet!" Risa put in.

"If the baby is a girl, *I* have to name her," I said. "Maybe I should hope for a boy, too."

"Don't worry," Megan said. "We'll help you think of a good name."

"Right," Nikki agreed. She thought for a second. "How about Relevé Ruiz?"

The rest of us groaned.

"Out of the question," I said.

"I've got it!" Megan said. "Darci Kistler Ruiz."

"It's been used," I pointed out. (Darci Kistler is a famous ballerina.)

"How about Risa Ruiz?" Risa suggested.

"Risa?" I asked, making a face. "Yuck!"

Risa stuck her tongue out at me. Then she smiled.

I turned to Becky. "Do you have any ideas?" I asked.

But Becky had gotten that faraway look in her eyes. "A new baby," she said. "Your parents must be so happy."

"They are," I agreed. I was going to add "I'm happy, too." But then I thought of all the things Risa had said. She made babies seem pretty scary. I wasn't sure how happy I was anymore.

Six

Grown-up Worries

"Truth or dare?" Risa asked me. It was later that night, and we were all sitting around my bedroom.

"Dare," I said.

Have you ever played Truth or Dare? It's one of the best games ever invented. And it's perfect for slumber parties.

Here's how it works: You start by choosing one of the other players and asking her, "Truth or dare?" If she chooses dare, you make her do something shocking. If she chooses truth, you make her answer an embarrassing question. Next, whoever you picked gets a turn to ask someone else, "Truth or dare?" The game can go on for hours.

Risa bit her lip and thought about what she should make me do. "Kiss him!" she said, pointing to my poster of Nilas Martins.

I groaned. "Do I have to?"

"Yes!" my friends yelled together.

I got up. I walked over to the poster and gave Nilas a quick peck on the cheek.

"Boo!" Nikki shouted.

"That doesn't count!" Risa yelled. "Kiss him like you *love* him."

"Because you *do*!" Nikki added.

"Fine," I said. I made a kissy-kissy face at the poster. "Oh, Nilas," I said. "You're such a hunk!" I gave the poster a sloppy kiss right on the mouth.

"Woo!"

"All right!"

I ran back to my bed. My face was burning. "Megan, truth or dare?" I asked.

"Truth," Megan said.

I grinned. "Do you like Dean Stellar?" I asked.

"As a boyfriend," Risa added quickly.

"No," Megan said.

"Remember," Nikki said. "You have to tell the absolute truth."

Megan looked mad. And she almost *never* looks mad. "I wish you guys would stop it," she said. "I don't like Dean!"

"She's lying," I said. "Look at her face! It's turning red."

"You know the punishment for lying during Truth or Dare," Risa said with a serious face.

"Tickle attack!" Risa, Nikki, and I yelled together. We all jumped on Megan.

"Stop!" Megan squealed. She tried to wiggle away from us.

"Come on, Becky," I shouted. "Help us get her!"

"No," Becky said. "I believe Megan. Not everyone's boy crazy, you know."

"Everyone but *you* is," Nikki said.

Now Becky looked mad. "That's not true," she said. "Jillian doesn't like boys, either."

My mother poked her head into my room. "Bedtime," she announced.

We all groaned. But I got into bed, and my friends crawled into their sleeping bags.

Mom flipped off the light. "Good night," she said.

"Good night," we answered.

Mom closed the door so that it was open only a crack.

My parents let me have lots of slumber parties during the summer. They have a rule that my friends and I have to be in bed by midnight. It's not such a bad rule. Midnight is three whole hours past my regular bedtime. If I stay up much later, I'm sleepy the whole next day.

"Megan," I whispered in the dark. "Don't be mad."

"I don't like Dean," Megan insisted.

"Okay, okay," I told her.

"Becky, are you mad?" Nikki whispered.

"No," Becky said.

I believed Becky. But I didn't believe Megan. Anyone can see she likes Dean. But I was too tired to argue about it. I closed my eyes. A few seconds later I was sound asleep.

I woke up in the middle of the night. All of my friends were asleep. My clock said 2:06.

I knew what woke me up. My stomach. It was growling like an angry bear.

My stomach drives me crazy. No matter how much I eat, it isn't enough. I grew two inches and an entire shoe size last year. I'll probably be six feet tall by the time I'm twelve. I wish I were more like Megan. She hasn't grown at all since the beginning of third grade. She's tiny and adorable.

I tried to go back to sleep. I counted sheep, but the furry animals kept turning into fluffy pieces of fudge.

Fudge. Yum. My mother had helped me and my friends make fudge that evening. There was still a lot left. I decided to go down to the kitchen and get a piece.

I eased out of bed and tiptoed toward the door.

I was most of the way there when Becky sat up. She's a light sleeper.

"What time is it?" Becky mumbled.

"It's late," I whispered. "I'm going to get a snack."

Becky pulled her legs out of her sleeping bag. "Wait for me," she said. "I was dreaming about fudge. I want a piece." (Becky has grown a lot this year, too.)

We crept into the hallway. But at the top of the stairs we stopped. Voices were coming from downstairs.

"Who's up?" Becky whispered.

"I don't know," I said. "Come on. Let's see."

Becky and I tiptoed down half the stairs. We sat down in the shadows, near the wall.

My mother and father were sitting at the dining room table. Dad had on sweats.

Mom was wearing her fuzzy blue bathrobe.

My parents were surrounded by papers. They were talking in quiet voices. They sounded worried.

I put a finger to my lips. Becky and I were very, very quiet. I was hardly breathing.

I heard Dad say "kids" and then "money."

Mom said "give up."

Becky motioned to me wildly. She tiptoed up

47

the stairs and I followed her. We stopped in the hallway outside my bedroom.

"I heard your mother say 'give up,'" Becky said. "I think your parents are going to give up your house! You're going to have to move."

"I didn't hear them say 'house,'" I told Becky.

"You're right," Becky said. "But they did say 'kids.' Maybe they're going to put you up for adoption!"

"Your imagination is freaking," I told Becky.

"Listen," Becky said. "If your parents have to give you up, I'll make my mother adopt you."

I giggled. "You're crazy!"

"We'll see," Becky said.

We heard footsteps on the stairs.

Becky and I ran into my room. I got into bed, and Becky climbed back into her sleeping bag. My clock said 2:16. It was really, really late. But I had a hard time falling asleep. What had my parents been talking about? What if it was something terrible?

Seven

Diapers and Strained Peas

"Good morning," I said.

"Morning," Mom answered.

It was Saturday. My friends and I had just gotten up and trooped downstairs. Mom was sitting at the kitchen table. Alison and my dad were playing in my sister's room.

"What's for breakfast?" I asked Mom.

"Cereal," Mom said.

I wrinkled my nose. Cereal is not a nice breakfast for guests. But Mom looked tired. She *had* been up half the night. I decided not to argue with her.

I took out the boxes of cereal and passed them around to my friends. Then I went to the refrigerator to get the milk. I pushed aside some lettuce and peeked behind a bottle of carrot juice. "Mom," I said, "we're out of milk."

"We are? Well, I'll run down to the store and get some."

"I'll go," I offered.

"Thanks," Mom said, sounding relieved. She took her purse off the table. "Darn! I don't have any money. I'd better go to the store myself, Katie. Jodi will let me pay her on Monday." (Jodi is the woman who owns the store.)

As soon as Mom was gone, Becky pulled me aside. "This is worse than I thought," she whispered. "Your mother doesn't even have money for milk!"

I was still hoping Becky's imagination was going wild. But I was beginning to wonder . . .

"What should I do?" I whispered.

"You have to ask your parents what's going on," Becky said.

"Hey, what's wrong, you guys?" Risa asked.

Becky and I turned around. Risa, Nikki, and Megan were staring at us. They looked worried.

"It's my parents," I explained. "Becky and I saw them having a *serious* talk last night."

"About what?" Nikki asked.

"Money, I think," I said. "But I have to be sure. I'm going to ask my mom as soon as she gets home."

"Maybe we should go," Megan suggested.

"What about breakfast?" Nikki asked. "I'm hungry."

"You can eat at home," Megan said in a no-nonsense voice. "Katie needs some time alone with her parents. Right, Katie?"

"Well . . ." I said. I didn't want to kick my friends out. But I did think it was a good idea for them to leave.

"Let's go," Megan said. She led the others upstairs. They packed up and took off in record time.

When Mom got back from the store, she found me staring at five bowls of dry cereal. I was trying not to cry.

"Where is everyone?" she asked.

"They went home," I explained. "Mom, I know something's wrong. Please tell me what it is."

She gave me a weak smile. "It sure is hard to hide things from you," she said. "Go on into the living room. I'll get Ali and your dad. We'll have a family meeting."

A few minutes later Mom, Dad, Alison, and I were all gathered in the living room.

"Your mother and I had a long talk last night," Dad told us. "We realized that the new baby will mean lots of changes."

"What kind of changes?" I asked.

"For one thing, the two of you are going to have to share a room," Mom said. "We'd like to make your room the nursery, Katie, and have you move in with Alison."

"We're going to have fun!" Alison said.

I smiled at her. She was being sweet. But I wasn't crazy about the idea of giving up my room. I wouldn't have any privacy. And where would my friends sleep when I had slumber parties?

"When do I have to move?" I asked.

"The baby is due in February," Mom told me. "We can move your things during Christmas vacation."

Whew! Christmas vacation was months away. School hadn't even started yet. I had plenty of time to get used to the idea of giving up my room.

Dad must have noticed my relief. "There's more," he warned me.

Mom nodded. "When the baby is born, I'm going to stop working for about a year. There will be less money coming in. And we'll have doctor's bills to pay."

"There will also be lots of things to buy," Dad put in. "Diapers, clothes, food for the baby, lots of stuff."

"I could get a job," I offered.

"Me too," Alison said. (She's such a copycat.)

Mom and Dad laughed.

"That won't be necessary," Dad told us.

"Are you sure?" I said. "Mom didn't even have money for milk this morning."

"Oh, honey—" Mom said. "That was only because I forgot to go to the bank yesterday."

"I don't want you guys to worry," Dad added. "Things will be fine. We're just going to be more careful about how we spend money."

"Your father and I won't go to the movies as often," Mom said.

"And, Alison, I'm afraid you won't be able to take quite so many art classes," Dad put in.

Alison stuck out her bottom lip. I knew she was going to start crying any second.

"What about me?" I asked quickly.

Mom pulled Alison into her lap. "Well, we've noticed you haven't been enjoying your ballet classes much lately," she said. "We think a break would be good for you."

In a way my mother was right. I hadn't been enjoying ballet. But that was just because of Madame Trikilnova. The thought of giving up ballet made tears come to my eyes.

"It may just be for a little while," Dad told me. "You might be able to take classes again in a year or two. Until then you can still take modern dance at the recreation center."

"Could I quit modern instead?" I asked.

Dad shook his head. "Your modern dance class is much less expensive than ballet," he explained.

I took a deep breath. I didn't want to be a crybaby like Alison. Besides, my parents weren't really *asking* me to give up ballet. They were telling me I *had* to. That meant even if they knew I was unhappy, they couldn't change anything.

"Your ballet classes are paid for through the end of the summer session," Mom told me.

I did a quick count. I had six classes left. One of them started soon. I jumped up. "I've got to get going," I told my parents. "I don't want to be late to ballet."

Eight

Becky's Plan

I grabbed my stuff and ran to the ballet school. I got there early. Well, not exactly *early*. But early for me.

"What's wrong?" Becky asked as soon as I pushed opened the dressing room door.

I just stood there, trying to catch my breath.

"It must be something serious," Nikki said. "Katie has never been here this early before."

"Shh," Megan told Nikki. "Is it something serious, Katie?"

"I'm not allowed to—" I started.

Risa came in. "What's going on?" she asked.

"I'm not allowed to take ballet anymore," I blurted out. Then I started to cry. I hardly ever cry. My friends looked freaked out.

Becky put her arm around my shoulders.

"Don't cry," Megan begged. "Just tell us what happened."

I took a deep breath. "My parents don't have the money for lessons," I explained. "They have to save it for baby stuff."

"Babies can't be too expensive," Nikki said. "They're really small."

"And they don't eat anything," Becky put in. "All they need is a little milk."

Risa shook her head. "Sara has all sorts of special baby equipment," she told us. "Colette is always complaining about how expensive everything is."

"That's what my parents said, too," I agreed.

"What else did they say?" Becky asked.

I pulled my dance clothes out of my bag and started to get dressed. "They told me I have to give up my room," I said. "It's going to be the nursery."

My friends groaned.

"I have to share with Ali," I added.

Risa looked horrified.

"You can come over to my house whenever you need a break," Megan told me.

"Thanks," I said.

Madame Trikilnova poked her head into the dressing room. "What are you girls doing down here?" she demanded. "Your class has already started."

Becky gasped.

We all jumped up and ran upstairs. We burst

into Studio C. Charlotte, Lynn, and John gave us funny looks.

Pat greeted us with a big smile. "Good to see you," she said. "We weren't going to have much of a class without you."

"We didn't mean to be late," Becky said. "We're sorry."

"It's okay," Pat said. "Let's just get started."

Everyone took their places. I was in front of Megan and behind Nikki. I peeked into the mirror. My eyes were still red. I hoped it wasn't too apparent I had been crying.

Al began to play.

"Maybe your parents will change their minds," Megan whispered as we eased into a *plié*.

"I don't think they can," I whispered back. "Not unless they find some money."

"Maybe they'll win the lottery," Nikki whispered.

"They don't play the lottery," I pointed out.

"Nikki, please face front," Pat said. "Megan and Katie, pay attention. You're two beats behind everyone else."

I was embarrassed. Megan and I hadn't even noticed we were out of step.

We were quiet during the rest of the barre exercises. But as we got ready to start center work, Becky pulled me aside.

"Did your parents seem worried?" she whispered.

"A little," I told her.

"Should I ask my mom about adopting you?" Becky asked.

"I don't think—" I started.

"Katie, Becky," Pat said, "we can start as soon as you quiet down."

Becky and I stopped whispering and lined up facing front. Nikki, Megan, and Risa were right behind us.

"Why don't you drop modern?" Megan asked.

"Good idea," Risa said.

"Ballet *is* much more important," Nikki added. "All of your friends take ballet."

"I can't—" I started. I stopped talking because Al had stopped playing.

I looked up and saw Pat staring at us. She looked angry.

"Girls, I'm out of patience," Pat said. "First, you were late to class. You kept everyone waiting. Now you insist on whispering. Remember, you aren't the only people in this class. If you can't be quiet, I'll have to ask you to leave."

Becky was bright red.

I couldn't remember Pat using that tone of voice before. I felt bad we had made her angry.

"I'm sorry," I told Pat. "It was my fault. We'll be quiet. I promise."

My friends and I were quiet for the rest of class. When it was over, we clapped extra hard. We wanted Pat to know we were really sorry.

Becky rushed up to me.

"I'm sorry I got you in trouble," I told her.

Becky shook her head. "Don't worry about that," she said. "I have an idea! Why don't you come back to public school?"

"What does school have to do with anything?" I asked.

"We're talking about *money*," Becky explained. "Public school is free. And your private school—"

"Costs plenty!" I interrupted. "Becky, you're a genius."

Becky grinned. "I know," she said.

"I want to ask my parents right away," I said. "Come on!"

"Okay," Becky agreed.

"Where are you guys going?" Megan asked as we ran by her on the stairs.

"I'll explain later," I yelled to her.

Becky and I hurried downstairs and changed our clothes. We ran to my house. My parents were in the kitchen, cooking lunch. It smelled fabulous. I realized I hadn't eaten breakfast.

"Becky thought of a way I could still take ballet lessons!" I announced as we burst through the door. "You could send me back to public school."

Before I even finished talking, Mom and Dad were shaking their heads.

"I'm sorry, Katie," Mom said gently. "Your dad and I discussed this. We think you do better work at St. Anthony's. So that's where you're going to stay."

"But I like public school better," I said.

"It's out of the question," Mom replied.

"But—" I started.

"You heard your mother," Dad interrupted. "End of discussion."

Becky and I went upstairs. I kicked my door as hard as I could. I was furious.

"Don't be angry," Becky told me. "We'll think of something. I promise."

Nine

Ballerinas in Business

"So, do you guys have any brilliant ideas?" Becky asked.

It was Sunday. After going to church with my family, I met Becky, Risa, Nikki, and Megan at the coffee shop. Becky had told everyone to come for an emergency meeting.

Nikki was the only one of us who had any money. She was eating an order of french fries.

The coffee shop is next door to the ballet school. All of the kids in Glory love to hang out there. My friends and I even have a favorite booth. From it we can look out the window and spy on everyone walking down Main Street.

Remember Dean? The boy Megan says she doesn't like? Well, his parents own the coffee shop. Mr. and Mrs. Stellar are really cool.

Megan twisted around in her seat and glanced over her shoulder.

"That's the third time you've done that," Nikki said.

"Done what?" Megan asked.

"Looked around the restaurant," Nikki said.

"It is not," Megan protested. "Why would I look around the restaurant?"

"To see if Dean is here," I suggested.

Philip and Dean sometimes help their parents in the coffee shop. They usually do dishes or clear tables.

"I told you!" Megan yelled. "I don't like Dean!"

Mrs. Stellar was sitting behind the counter. She glanced over at us.

Megan slid down in her seat. "Will you guys please be quiet?" she asked angrily.

I giggled. "You're the one who's yelling."

Poor Megan. She was really red. I guess that was our fault. We did tease her a lot. But I couldn't help it. It was so much fun!

"Why do we always have to talk about boys?" Becky asked. "We're supposed to be figuring out a way for Katie to keep taking ballet lessons."

"Your parents won't send you back to public school?" Risa asked.

"They refuse," I told her.

"Well, I like having you at St. Anthony's," Risa said.

"Thanks," I said.

"There's only one thing for you to do," Nikki mumbled with her mouth full. "Pay for the lessons yourself."

"What a great idea!" Megan said.

"Yeah!" Becky said.

I shook my head. "It's not that great," I said. "I only have about two dollars in my piggy bank at home."

"Don't worry," Megan said. "You can earn the money. We'll help you. Right, guys?"

"Right!" Becky, Risa, and Nikki said together.

"Great!" I said.

We grinned at each other for a few minutes.

"So, um . . ." Risa looked uncomfortable. "What can we do? I mean, what will people *pay* us to do?"

I reached for a fry.

Nikki smacked my hand. "Too bad nobody will pay Katie to eat," she said.

"I can't help it if I'm always hungry." I grabbed the last fry on the plate and popped it into my mouth.

"Come on, you guys," Megan urged. "Think! What kind of job can we get?"

"How about a paper route?" Becky suggested.

"Forget it," Megan said. "My brother has been waiting for a paper route for two years. There's a long waiting list."

"Baby-sitting?" Risa suggested.

"My parents think I'm too young," Becky said.

"Mine too," I agreed.

"Well, what are we good at?" Megan asked. "Other than dancing, I mean."

"I can set the table in three minutes and twelve seconds," Becky said proudly.

"Mom says I'm good at vacuuming," Nikki said.

"I painted our bathroom," Risa put in.

"Last week I fixed the screen in our back door," Megan added.

"I've got it!" I announced. "We can do odd jobs."

"What are odd jobs?" Megan asked.

"It means we'll do whatever anyone asks us to," I explained. "You know, the kind of jobs our parents make us do. The stuff adults don't want to do themselves."

"That sounds perfect!" Becky said.

The others nodded.

"Then we're in business," I said.

Ten

Twenty-two Dollars

"Katie!" shouted a familiar voice on Monday morning.

"Up here," I yelled.

I heard footsteps on the stairs. A second later Becky and Megan burst into my room. (Becky never bothers to ring the doorbell at my house.)

"Look," I told them. "I made a sign for our new business."

"Let me see," Megan said.

I held up the sign. It said:

BALLERINAS IN BUSINESS
WE DO YOUR ODD JOBS,
YOU HAVE MORE TIME TO ENJOY THE SUMMER.
LOWEST PRICES

Underneath all that my name and phone number were listed. I had decorated the sign with drawings of mops and buckets, nails and hammers, paint cans and paintbrushes.

"Why does it say 'lowest prices'?" Becky asked. "If we charge a lot, we'll make more money."

I shook my head. "If we charge a lot, nobody will hire us."

The doorbell rang.

"That must be Risa and Nikki," Megan said. "Let's go!"

Becky, Megan, and I ran downstairs. Nikki and Risa were standing on my front porch. I showed them the sign. Then we all headed down to Main Street.

"Let's use the copy machine at the post office," I suggested.

"Wait," Megan said as we walked by the library. "Let's go see Ms. Bell. She can tell us what's going on in New York. And maybe she'll offer to make the copies for us."

"Good idea," Becky agreed.

Ms. Bell's office is in the same building as the library. Jillian's mother works with Jillian's grandfather, Mr. Bell. They're both lawyers. (That means they know a lot about the law. People pay them for their advice.)

We walked into the building and up to the second floor. Megan went up to a door and knocked.

"Come in!" a voice called from inside.

We walked into the serious-looking office. There were rows of big law books lining the wall. A fancy carpet covered the floor. Jillian's mother was working on a computer. Several framed certificates hung above her head.

Ms. Bell looked up when we came in. "Hi," she said with a grin. "What are you girls up to?"

"We're going into business," I said. I showed her the sign.

Ms. Bell studied it for a second. "Looks good," she said.

"We were going to make copies at the post office," Megan put in. "We just stopped by to ask you how Jillian is doing."

Ms. Bell stood up. "I'll copy the sign for you," she offered. "It will save you a little money."

"Thanks!" I said. I had planned to spend a dollar on copies. Now I wouldn't have to. That was one less dollar we had to earn.

Ms. Bell took my sign. She walked over to the copy machine and pushed some buttons. The machine started to spit out copies.

"Heather is going to move in with Jillian and her dad this afternoon," Ms. Bell reported. "Jillian is really excited. She said it's going to be like having a big sister."

"It sounds like she's having fun," Megan said.

"I think she is," Ms. Bell said. She handed me a stack of copies. "Good luck with your business."

"Thanks!" I said.

We hurried downstairs. We walked down Main Street. Megan handed a sign to everyone who passed. The rest of us went into stores and asked if we could hang a sign in the window.

"Hi, Mrs. Stellar," I said, walking into the coffee shop. "May I hang this up?"

Mrs. Stellar finished making change for a customer. Then she turned to me.

"Sure," she answered. "I'll give you a piece of tape. Why don't you put it up in the front window?"

"Thanks," I said. I put my stack of copies down on the counter. Then I went to hang up a sign.

Mrs. Stellar picked up another copy and read it. "I have a job for you," she told me. "We have two garbage cans full of stuff that can be recycled. I'll give you five dollars to sort it out."

"Great!" I said. "Can we do it now?"

"The sooner, the better," Mrs. Stellar said.

I went outside and got my friends. Mrs. Stellar led us into the kitchen of the coffee shop. She gave me a bunch of plastic bags.

"Put the clear glass in one bag," Mrs. Stellar told us. "The green glass goes into another bag. And the brown glass belongs in another one."

70

We nodded.

"Use a separate bag for foil," Mrs. Stellar went on. "Another one for plastic. Some newspapers might have gotten in with the cans by mistake. If you find any, put them in that corner."

"Whew," Nikki said after Mrs. Stellar had gone. "I never knew garbage was so complicated."

"I bet Dean and Philip have to do this all the time," Megan said.

"Only, they don't get paid," Risa added.

Becky held her nose as she picked up a sticky glass jar. "Poor Dean and Philip," she said.

"I wonder how the twins like football camp," I said.

Megan shrugged. "Who cares?"

Risa and I traded glances. I bit my lip to stop myself from laughing.

Sorting garbage is a disgusting job. My friends complained the entire time we were working. But they didn't quit. When we were finished, we washed our dirty hands in the restaurant's big metal sink. Then we went back out front.

"We're finished!" I announced.

"Great," Mrs. Stellar said. She pushed a button, and the register opened with a ding. "Should I give you each a dollar?"

"No," Becky said. "Katie gets all the money."

The rest of my friends nodded.

71

Mrs. Stellar took a five-dollar bill out of the register. She handed it to me, and I put it in my pocket. When we got out onto the sidewalk, everyone was grinning.

"This is going to be fun," Becky said.

"Every store on Main Street has a sign," I reported. "Where should we go now?"

"Cedar Street," Nikki suggested.

"Sounds good," I agreed.

The houses on Cedar Street are huge. The richest people in town live there.

Jillian lives on Cedar with her mother and grandparents. When we got to her house, Jillian's grandmother was sitting on the front porch.

"Hi, Mrs. Bell," we all yelled.

"Hi, girls," she called back.

I ran up and gave Mrs. Bell a sign. After she read it, she asked us to turn over her compost heap.

A compost heap is a pile of old leaves, eggshells, orange peels, apple cores, and who knows what else. If you let everything in the heap rot for a while, it turns into something that's good for your garden.

Mrs. Bell promised to pay us ten whole dollars. She gave us a shovel to share. Then she pointed us toward the corner of the garden.

"This is going to be easy," I said, running to the top of the pile.

But it wasn't easy.

On top the leaves were light. But as we dug deeper, the leaves got wetter. Wet leaves are heavy! Deeper down the compost looked like soil. It weighed a ton.

After working for about three minutes, I was all sweaty. I passed the shovel to Becky.

"Your turn," I gasped.

Becky took a turn. Then Nikki. And then Risa.

"How long do you think we should do this?" Megan asked. She leaned on the shovel. She was trying to catch her breath after digging for about four minutes.

"I don't know," I admitted. "Ten dollars is a lot."

"My sister earns two dollars an hour baby-sitting," Becky told us.

Risa's jaw dropped. "Do you think we have to dig for five hours?" she asked.

"We'd die," Nikki said with a groan.

Just then Mrs. Bell came outside. She walked toward us.

Megan went back to digging.

"We were just taking a little break," I told Mrs. Bell when she got close.

Mrs. Bell looked at the compost heap and at all of our sweaty faces. "You've done plenty," she told us. "This looks great!"

"Really?" Nikki said, sounding relieved.

"Really," Mrs. Bell said. She pulled a ten-dollar bill out of her pocket and handed it to me.

"Whoopee," I yelled as we left the Bells. "We've already made fifteen dollars! If you count the two dollars from my piggy bank, that makes seventeen dollars."

My friends and I walked back to Main Street. We sat down on the bench in front of the bank. I passed out sandwiches my mother had made that morning. We also had apples and a bag of oatmeal cookies.

We had almost finished eating when Mr. Byrne came down the street. Mr. Byrne is ancient. He and his friend Mr. Frantz always sit on the bank bench in the afternoons.

It took Mr. Byrne a long time to shuffle down the street.

"Good afternoon, ladies," he greeted us.

"Hi, Mr. Byrne," Megan said.

Becky jumped up. "You can sit here."

Mr. Byrne settled himself on the bench. "Saw your sign," he told me. "I'd like you to do my shopping for me. I'll pay you three dollars. Here's the list and the money."

I gulped down the last cookie and took the list from Mr. Byrne's wrinkled hand.

"Thanks!" I told him.

We all went down the street to the store. We

bought the things on Mr. Byrne's list. Then we took the bag of groceries and Mr. Byrne's change back to the bench.

By that time Mr. Frantz had arrived. He seemed to like our arrangement with Mr. Byrne, so he hired us to buy his groceries, too. He paid us the same amount Mr. Byrne had.

"We've made twenty-one dollars," I said. "It's unbelievable!"

"I've got to get home," Megan announced.

"Me too," Nikki put in.

"What are you guys doing tomorrow?" I asked.

Megan shrugged. "More odd jobs, I guess."

The others agreed. We would spend the next day working.

Becky and I headed toward home. On the way we passed a woman and her little boy. They were standing in their front yard. The boy was about three years old. He was sobbing.

"What's the matter?" I asked. The lady's face looked familiar, but I didn't know her name.

"Bobby's kitten climbed that tree," she told me. "Now she's afraid to come down."

"I'll get her," I volunteered.

"Could you?" the woman asked. "She's not too high."

"No problem," I told her.

"Katie's good at climbing trees," Becky put in.

I climbed the tree. I sat down on the same branch as the kitten. She was gray, with a white nose.

"Here, kitty, kitty, kitty," I called.

The cat made a tiny frightened meow.

I held a hand out toward her. But she wouldn't come any closer. Her claws were all the way out. She was holding on to the tree as tightly as she could.

I inched closer. I reached my hand under the kitten's belly and pulled her off the tree. She dug her claws into my hands and hung on. Since she was so little, her claws weren't strong. It didn't hurt much.

I backed down the tree. When I got close enough, I handed the kitten to Bobby's mother.

Bobby was grinning. "Thank you!"

I jumped out of the tree.

"Thanks so much," Bobby's mother said. "Please take this," she added, pulling a dollar bill out of her pocket.

"Thanks!" I said. Now we had earned twenty-two dollars! I felt rich. I could hardly wait until the next day.

Eleven

Quitters

"Hello?" I said.

The telephone had rung while I was eating breakfast on Tuesday. I swallowed a mouthful of toast before I answered it.

"Kadee?" came a voice. "I'b gob a coad."

"Who is this?" I asked.

"Risa," the stuffed-up-sounding voice replied.

I laughed. "Well, go back to bed. You sound terrible."

Poor Risa. Being sick in the summertime is the worst.

The phone rang again while I was getting dressed.

I pulled my T-shirt the rest of the way on. Then I ran for the phone in the hallway.

"Hello?" I said.

"Hi, Katie! This is Nikki."

"What's up?" I asked.

"Mom is taking me shopping in Seattle," Nikki announced. "We're going to be gone all day. So I can't do odd jobs."

"Oh," I said.

"Sorry," Nikki told me. "I told Mom I had plans. But she really wants me to go."

I noticed Nikki sounded pretty excited. That made me mad.

Two of my friends had quit already. Any minute, Megan and Becky would probably call and say *they* weren't coming, either.

I went to my bedroom and put on my gym shoes. I didn't care if everyone else quit. I was still going to do odd jobs.

"Katie!"

I ran into the hallway and peered over the railing. Megan and Becky were standing in the front hall.

"You're here!" I greeted them.

"We said we would be," Megan said.

I started down the stairs. "Nikki and Risa aren't coming."

"You look mad," Megan said.

"I am, a little," I admitted.

"Don't worry," Becky told me. "We'll get lots of jobs without them."

"I guess," I said.

"Let's go," Megan suggested. "You'll cheer up as soon as we start working."

Megan, Becky, and I went outside. The others waited on the sidewalk while I put a sign under every door on my street. Then we went down to Main Street.

"Where is everyone?" Becky wondered out loud.

For summer, it was a cool day. It was also overcast, foggy, and drizzling. Glory was practically empty. Everyone seemed to be shut up in their houses.

All the stores on Main Street were already displaying one of my signs.

"Maybe I should tape some signs to the trees," I said.

Megan squinted up at the sky. "They'll just get soggy."

"You're right," I said.

Ms. Eide, the librarian, came out of the post office. I ran to catch up with her.

"Do you have any odd jobs you'd like us to do?" I skipped backward in front of her.

"Not right now, Katie," Ms. Eide said. "But I'll call you if I think of anything."

I stopped skipping. "Thanks," I said as she passed.

Mr. Stellar was sweeping the sidewalk in front of the coffee shop.

Becky ran up to him. "We could do that."

"No, thanks," Mr. Stellar said. "I like to do this job myself. It gives me some time outside."

Becky and Megan looked glum. I felt the same way. We crossed the street and walked back the way we came.

"There's Charlotte," Becky said.

Charlotte came out of the video rental store. She was walking toward us.

"Hi!" Becky greeted her.

Charlotte didn't answer Becky. "I saw one of your signs," she told me. She sounded as if it were the silliest thing she had ever seen. "What are you going to do next? Open a lemonade stand?"

The three of us walked right past Charlotte and kept going. I was fuming. Charlotte is so spoiled. She'll probably never have to work for anything she wants.

"Why does she have to be so mean?" Becky asked.

"Forget her," Megan suggested.

We didn't say anything for a few minutes.

"Have you found a good girl's name yet?" Megan asked me.

"No," I said. "I've been too busy worrying

80

about my ballet lessons. Besides—" I stopped talking.

"What?" Becky asked.

"I don't want to think of a baby's name!" I exploded. "I hate that stupid baby. It's messing up everything!"

Megan and Becky traded looks.

I felt ashamed. I was really being mean. I'm a terrible person sometimes.

The rest of the morning was awful. It started to rain harder. The few people we saw didn't want to hire us.

Around noon we decided to take a break. We went to Becky's for lunch. When we got there, the Hills' house was shaking. Sophie, Becky's sister, was blasting her favorite CD.

"Come on in!" Becky yelled. "I'll make sandwiches."

"Hi!" Sophie yelled when we walked into the kitchen. She was reading a magazine at the kitchen table.

We all yelled hello back.

"We came to eat lunch," Becky shouted.

"What are you guys making?" Sophie yelled.

"Sandwiches!" Megan yelled. "We'll make one for you, too."

"Thanks!" Sophie yelled.

Becky and Megan danced to the music as they started to fix our food.

I sat down at the table. I didn't feel like cooking or dancing. I was too sad.

"How's your business going?" Sophie asked.

I leaned close to her so that she could hear. "We've made twenty-two dollars so far." Just saying "twenty-two dollars" made me feel great.

"Is that all?" Sophie asked.

"We've only been working for a day and a half," I reminded Sophie. "It isn't easy to earn twenty-two dollars."

"I know," Sophie said. "It's just that ballet lessons are super expensive."

Sophie got out of her chair. She dug around in a drawer until she found a flyer from Madame Trikilnova's.

Becky turned down the music.

Sophie sat down and opened the flyer. Becky, Megan, and I looked at it over her shoulder.

"Let me find the price for Intermediates," Sophie said. She ran her finger down a list of prices. "Here it is. The fall session costs four hundred and ten dollars."

"Wow!" Becky said.

Megan shook her head.

"No wonder my parents want me to quit," I said.

Sophie nodded. "Four hundred dollars is major money."

Becky put the sandwiches on the table and got a bag of potato chips out of the closet.

Usually I love to eat at Becky's. My parents never let me eat junk like potato chips. But I didn't feel hungry anymore.

"Well, we might as well quit doing odd jobs," I said. "We'll never earn enough."

"I think we should keep trying," Becky said.

"Me too," Megan said. "It will take us a long time to earn the money. But I still think we can do it."

"We have to do it," Becky told me. "Ballet wouldn't be the same without you."

"Don't give up," Sophie put in.

I smiled. "Okay," I said. "I won't." I was relieved my friends didn't want to quit. Doing odd jobs wasn't much fun. It was cool that they wanted to help.

I took a big bite of my sandwich. And then another. I was actually pretty hungry.

"What's for dessert?" I asked when my sandwich was gone.

The others laughed. I like to eat dessert with every meal.

"I think we have some cookies," Sophie said.

Megan got the bag out of the closet.

I was biting into my second chocolate-chip cookie when the phone rang.

Becky got it. "Hill residence," she said. "Hi! You did? We had the music on loud. Hang on a second." Becky moved her mouth away from the telephone. "Hillary just tried to call us three times. I think the music was so loud we couldn't hear the phone!"

"Oops," Sophie said.

Megan and I laughed.

Becky turned back to the phone. "What are you doing? Sounds cool. Katie and Megan are here, too. Okay. Let me ask them."

"What's up?" Megan asked.

"Hillary wants us to come over to her house," Becky explained. "She rented a video of *Pete's Universe III*."

Hillary Widmer was in Becky and Megan's class in regular school last year. I know Hillary, too. Everyone knows everyone in Glory.

I shook my head. "We can't go," I said. "We only have a few hours more to work before ballet class."

Megan and Becky traded glances.

"What's the matter?" I demanded.

Becky shrugged. "It's just that I really want to see the new *Pete's Universe*."

"Me too," Megan said. "I heard it was really funny."

"I thought you wanted to do odd jobs!" I exclaimed.

"I do," Becky insisted. "But fall session doesn't start for almost a month."

"We have lots of time to earn the money," Megan put in.

I was furious. My friends promised to stick by me. And two chocolate-chip cookies later, they change their minds!

"Fine," I yelled. "Go watch a movie. See if I care!"

"Katie," Becky said, "don't freak out."

"If it's important to you, we won't go," Megan added.

"No," I said. "Go! I'll earn the money without you."

I picked up another cookie and stomped toward the door.

"What should we do?" I heard Megan ask Becky.

"Give her time to cool off," Becky replied.

Twelve

A Bad Scare

"Mom and Dad got me into this mess," I mumbled.

Halfway home I decided I shouldn't be mad at *just* Becky and Megan. It was true that they wouldn't help me earn the money I needed. But it wasn't their fault I didn't have the money in the first place.

I rushed the rest of the way home. I was in a hurry to give Dad a piece of my mind. (Mom wouldn't be home yet. I planned to give her a piece of my mind at dinner.)

I threw open the door to my house.

Something was wrong. I knew it immediately.

My dad should have been at the computer in his study. Instead he was pacing the kitchen floor.

He looked up as I came in. "Katie!" he exclaimed. "Thank God you're home."

"What's the matter?" I asked.

"Your mother had to leave work about an hour ago," he told me. "She went to the hospital. Helen called to tell me."

Helen is Becky's mother. She works at the same company as my mother.

I felt dizzy. "Is she okay?" I whispered.

"She's probably fine. But we have to get to the hospital. Run upstairs and get Alison. I'll be in the car."

"Okay," I agreed.

I ran upstairs.

Alison was in her art nook. She was painting.

My little sister loves to do messy, creative stuff. The art nook is a special corner of her bedroom. There's a plastic table, and a plastic sheet on the floor. My parents put it together so that Alison could make as big a mess as she wanted.

"Hi, Katie!" Alison greeted me.

"Hi," I said. "Come on. We have to go pick up Mom."

"Where is she?" Alison asked.

"At the hospital," I said.

"Should I wash my hands first?" Alison asked. She sounded cheerful. Being six has its advantages. I wished I was young enough not to worry. Alison held up her hands for me to see. They were covered with paint.

"Wash them," I decided. "But be fast. We have to hurry."

Little kids are really slow. It took Alison *forever* to wash her hands. But finally she was ready to go. We ran downstairs. I helped her into the backseat of the car.

I climbed into the front.

We zoomed off toward the hospital.

"Where were you?" Dad asked me. "I searched for you all over Glory. I called all your friends."

"I was at Becky's," I said.

"I tried there," Dad told me. "Nobody answered."

"Really?" I thought for a minute. "We had the music on loud. Maybe we didn't hear the phone."

I glanced into the backseat. Alison was singing along with a Tots Tunes tape that was playing. She wasn't paying any attention to what my dad and I were saying.

"What happened to Mom?" I whispered.

"Helen said it had something to do with the baby," Dad told me. He smiled bravely. "I don't want you to worry. Everything is going to be fine."

"Okay," I said. But I didn't really believe my dad. *He* looked worried.

A few minutes later Dad parked the car at the hospital. We went inside and took the elevator to the birth and delivery department. Dad told a nurse behind a desk why we were there. She promised to keep an eye on Alison and me.

Dad went off to find Mom.

I watched him disappear down a long hallway.

"You girls can wait in our special waiting room," the nurse said. She pointed to a room with brightly colored plastic chairs. "There are lots of toys in here."

"Thank you," I told her. I took Alison's hand and led her into the waiting room. I helped her pick out a puzzle to do.

I chose a magazine and sat down.

Alison settled on the floor, at my feet. She started to fit the puzzle pieces together. At the same time she tried out baby names.

"Ralph R. Ruiz," Alison said in a singsong voice. "Ronnie R. Ruiz. Toys R. Ruiz."

I tried to read, but I couldn't. I was worried about my mother and the baby.

I sighed.

Alison turned around and studied my face. "What's wrong?" she asked.

I made myself smile. "Everything's fine," I said, trying to sound happy.

Alison turned back to her puzzle. She was too young to understand. But I knew sometimes babies died before they were even born.

I closed my eyes. *Dear God,* I prayed. *Please let my mother and the baby be okay. If you do, I'll never complain about giving up my ballet classes ever again.*

When I opened my eyes, Dad was coming back down the hall. Mom was with him!

I jumped up. I wanted to throw my arms around Mom, but I didn't. I didn't want to hurt her.

"Is everything okay?" I asked.

"Everything's great," Mom told me. "I just have to stay in bed for a few days."

"How's the baby?" I asked.

"The baby's fine," Mom said.

"That's terrific!" I said, and meant it.

I vowed to keep my side of my deal with God.

Thirteen

Cold Muscles

As soon as we got home, Mom changed into her nightgown. She crawled into bed.

Dad moved the television and VCR into my parents' bedroom. I brought up that day's paper and found Mom's reading glasses.

"Thank you, Katie," Mom said. "I'm going to read this later. Right now I want to take a little nap."

Before I could reply, she sat up and glanced at the clock on her bedside table. "Katie, look at the time!" she said.

"Oh, no," I said. "My ballet class has already started."

"You can skip class if you want," Dad said. He looked too worn out to argue with me.

"No, thanks," I said. "I want to go." I got my dancing gear and headed toward the ballet school. I was very, very late.

I ran all the way. In the dressing room I changed twice as fast as Becky does. Then I took the stairs to the second floor two at a time.

"Mrrw!" A ball of fur jumped sideways in front of me. I hadn't seen Giselle sitting on the steps. I think I stepped on one of her paws.

"Sorry, Giselle!" I yelled.

I kept running—down the hall and through the door of Studio C.

"I know I'm late," I said as soon as I pushed the door open. "I'm really sorry, but my mother—"

I stopped talking. Everyone was staring at me.

Becky looked horrified. She was making a sign that I should be quiet.

I spun around to face Pat. But Pat wasn't there. Madame Trikilnova was. She had her arms crossed, and she was glaring at me. She did not look friendly.

"Katie, you have interrupted my class," Madame Trikilnova said sternly. "I do not understand what you are doing here at all. You are very late. You have already missed all of the barre."

"But I—"

"I'm sorry," Madame Trikilnova said. (She didn't sound sorry.) "You cannot join the class now. You are not properly warmed up."

"What should I do?" I asked.

92

"Leave," Madame Trikilnova said.

I stared at her. Then I turned and banged out of the studio.

Giselle was sitting in the hallway, licking her paw. Giselle and I are usually friends. But she didn't even look up at me. I figured she was angry that I had stepped on her.

What a terrible day. Even the cat was mad at me.

Fourteen

A Dreadful Class

"I might die before this is over," I told Becky.

It was Thursday. Becky and I were in the dressing room, getting ready for class. Pat was away at a workshop in Seattle. Madame Trikilnova was going to teach our class again that afternoon.

Becky gave me an understanding smile. "I expected you to skip," she told me. "Madame Trikilnova was hard on you last class."

"I considered skipping," I admitted.

"Why did you come?" Becky asked.

"I only have four classes left," I explained. "I don't want to miss any of them."

"Don't say that," Becky said. "We'll earn the money for your classes."

"I really don't think we can," I told her.

"We can too!" Becky insisted.

Lynn and Charlotte came into the dressing room.

94

"Hi," Lynn said.

Charlotte wrinkled her nose at my legs.

I glanced down. My tights had a run in them. That was nothing unusual. Tights rip easily. Most of the Pinks wore tights with runs in them. But not Charlotte. Hers were always perfect. What a snob.

"I'm ready to go up," I told Becky.

"Me too," Becky said.

We pushed open the door and went into the hall. Nikki and Risa were on their way into the dressing room.

"How come you're here so early?" Risa asked, looking shocked.

"I want to be on time," I explained. "I'm not going to do anything to make Madame Trikilnova angry today."

Becky and I walked into Studio C.

Madame Trikilnova was already there. "I see you decided to come on time," she greeted me. "I am honored."

I felt like yelling at her. Madame Trikilnova wasn't being fair. I had been late for a good reason. And she hadn't even let me explain.

"Good afternoon," I said sweetly.

Becky and I started stretching out. We were the only kids in the studio. Madame Trikilnova watched every move we made. Usually my friends and I joke around before class. But with Madame Trikilnova watching, Becky and I were too nervous to have fun.

Finally Charlotte and Lynn came in.

"Whew," Becky whispered to me.

"I've never been so happy to see Charlotte," I whispered.

Al arrived.

Madame Trikilnova nodded at him.

Al nodded back. He looked nervous.

Megan and Nikki and Risa came in.

John hurried in.

The instant Madame Trikilnova saw him, she clapped her hands. "We will begin!" she announced.

Everyone scrambled for a place at the barre.

Megan grabbed my arm. "Stand in front of me," she whispered. "I don't want Madame Trikilnova to see me."

"Okay," I agreed. I took a place in front of Megan and behind Risa.

Madame Trikilnova made an angry gesture. "What are you children thinking?" she demanded. "That is not how you line up! Tall people belong in back. How can I see you if you are all in a jumble?"

Madame Trikilnova stormed down the center of the studio. She looked like a stale prune. "Miss Isozaki, Miss Ruiz is blocking you. I want you up front."

Megan walked toward the front of the studio. She looked panicked. Poor Megan. She hates to dance in the front.

"Miss Stype, you are the tallest in the class," Madame Trikilnova said. "Please stand in the back."

Charlotte's eyes went wide with fury.

I grinned.

Charlotte is a big show-off. She always stands in the front of the studio, where everyone can see her.

"Miss Ruiz, you are the second tallest," Madame Trikilnova added. "Stand in front of Miss Stype."

I stopped grinning. I didn't want to stand anywhere near Charlotte. I'm telling you, growing is a curse. I had to stand near the Monster because I was so tall.

Madame Trikilnova studied the class with a frown. She gave us a satisfied nod, and showed us the exercise she wanted us to do. (*Pliés,* of course!)

As we danced, Madame Trikilnova clapped loudly with the beat. "Watch your bottoms!" she yelled. "They are sticking out. Tuck them in. You should look swans—not ducks!"

I giggled.

"Ms. Ruiz," Madame Trikilnova said. "You do not have time to laugh. Your arm looks like spaghetti. It's sagging. Hold it up!"

Madame Trikilnova marched to the front of the

studio. She signaled for Al to stop playing. "I want you to do a *grand plié* in eight counts." She did one of the slow *pliés*. "You have plenty of time to make it perfect."

The class started the exercise.

Madame Trikilnova walked up and down the studio. She patted Nikki on the bottom. "Tuck it in!" she demanded.

I had to bite my lip to keep from laughing.

We made it through *tendus, dégagés*, and a few other exercises without too much trouble. But the *ronds de jambe en l'air* were trouble.

Ronds de jambe en l'air are difficult. Pat usually has us do four sets of four *ronds de jambe* with each leg. The exercise goes like this: We start with our left hands on the barre. We lift our right legs straight out to the side, then draw four circles in the air with our toes. Then we get to put our legs down for a couple of counts. (They're tired!) Then—*zing!*—our legs go back up again, and we draw four circles going the other way. And then we repeat the whole thing from the beginning before turning to the other side. Everyone is always very happy when the *ronds de jambe* are finished. They hurt.

"We will repeat the entire exercise," Madame Trikilnova announced when we finished.

The whole class, including Charlotte, groaned.

Halfway through, I started to get really tired. Tears came to my eyes.

"Miss Ruiz," Madame Trikilnova said. "You are getting lazy! Hold your thigh up high."

"But my leg is exhausted," I admitted.

I immediately knew I shouldn't have talked back.

Madame Trikilnova looked furious. "The rest of you can take a break," she told the class. "Miss Ruiz, you will begin the exercise over again."

Charlotte giggled.

With everyone watching, I was too proud to be lazy. I forced myself to keep my legs up high. It was hard. By the time I finished, both legs were shaking.

We started to move into places for center work.

"Good job," Becky whispered to me.

She was trying to cheer me up. I didn't feel too cheery. Madame Trikilnova really was trying to kill me.

One of the last exercises we did in the center was *développés*. *Développés* take a lot of strength. Usually I'm good at them. But that afternoon my legs were just too tired.

"Turnout!" Madame Trikilnova yelled at me. "Turnout! Use your stomach muscles!"

After center work was finished, Madame Trikilnova showed us a combination. I started to

relax. I can usually do combinations after seeing them once.

Megan, Risa, and I were in the same group. We lined up and started to dance. I just wanted to finish and get out of there. But we had danced only a few steps when Madame Trikilnova clapped her hands.

Al stopped playing.

"Miss Ruiz," Madame Trikilnova said. "Where are your arms supposed to go on two?"

"Um . . ." I said.

"Well?" Madame Trikilnova demanded.

"I don't know," I admitted.

"Miss Cumberland?" Madame Trikilnova asked.

"Fifth position *en bas*," Risa said shyly. (That means your hands are in front of your body, with your elbows slightly bent.) Risa sounded sorry that she knew.

"That is correct," Madame Trikilnova said. "Do it again."

Risa, Megan, and I moved back. I tried to keep my mind on my dancing, but it was hard. I was so angry. Why was Madame Trikilnova picking on me? I wasn't dancing worse than anyone else.

Megan, Risa, and I prepared for a *pirouette*.

This is so unfair! I told myself. At that second I lost my balance. I fell sideways and bumped into Risa.

"Stop!" Madame Trikilnova demanded. "Begin again. Miss Ruiz, you don't seem ready to do a *pirouette*. After the preparation, I want you to come up onto demi-pointe. But do not turn. Miss Cumberland and Miss Isozaki will do the *pirouette* without you."

My face was burning.

Risa, Megan, and I began again. When it was time for the *pirouette*, I didn't turn. I went up onto demi-pointe and tried to smile. I didn't want Madame Trikilnova to know how mad she had made me.

"We are out of time," Madame Trikilnova announced when we finished.

Everyone started to clap. I told myself I was only clapping for Al.

"Whew," Megan said. "I'm glad that's over."

We headed for the door as quickly as possible.

"You disappointed me today," Madame Trikilnova said as I left the studio. "You need to work much harder."

I felt ashamed—and sad. I had only three classes left. There wasn't much time for me to work harder.

Fifteen

A Good Deal

"All right, Mom!" Alison yelled.

"Woo! Woo! Woo!" I yelled.

Dad sat back and clapped his hands.

"Thanks," Mom said. She sat down at the kitchen table. "But I don't deserve cheers. All I did was come downstairs for breakfast."

It was Saturday morning. Mom had spent the last three days in bed. I had done everything I could to make her comfortable. I brought her breakfast and lunch, magazines and the mail. The doctor had said she could get out of bed that morning. I was glad. All that helping was exhausting.

"I cooked breakfast for you," Alison announced.

"Great," Mom said. "What are we having?"

"Cereal!"

Mom, Dad, and I laughed.

"What's so funny?" Alison asked. She passed

the cereal box around the table.

"Nothing," I said. I got up and took the milk out of the refrigerator.

"Oh, thanks," Alison said. "I forgot about the milk."

Dad winked at me. "What should we do today?" he asked.

"Let Mom decide!" Alison said.

Mom thought for a second. "Well, we gave away Alison's baby stuff years ago," she said. "Maybe we should go shopping for a crib. Helen told me Eva's is having a sale." (Eva's is a store at the mall. It sells stuff for babies.)

"That sounds like fun," Alison decided. She loves to shop.

I thought a crib sounded like a boring thing to buy. Besides, we had about six months to get one. (Mom is a plan-ahead type.) But I didn't complain. I was in a terrific mood. It was wonderful to have my mother back again.

As soon as we finished breakfast, we all piled into the car. Dad drove to the mall and parked in front of Eva's.

We went inside and looked at the cribs.

Alison found one that was really great. It was painted white. One side slid up and down on tracks. That was so you wouldn't hurt your back picking up a heavy baby.

"It's perfect," Dad said. "But I'm afraid it costs too much, even on sale."

Mom didn't give up. She calmly examined several of the same kind of crib. She found one with chipped paint. She called a salesman over and showed him the bad spot.

"I'll give you thirty percent off," the salesman told us.

"Perfect," Mom said. "We'll take it."

On the way home we stopped at the hardware store. Mom and I picked out a can of paint. The paint cost two dollars. The deal Mom made at Eva's saved us thirty-eight dollars. Even after buying the paint, we had saved thirty-six dollars. That's a lot of money!

At home Dad took the chipped piece of the crib out of the box. He carried it down into the basement. I helped him paint the chipped spot. It only took a few minutes.

Just as we were finishing, the phone rang. It was Becky. I told her all about my morning.

"Your mother is so smart," Becky said.

"I know," I agreed.

"Too bad you can't get a discount on your ballet lessons," Becky said.

"Becky!" I exclaimed. "Maybe I *can*!"

"You've got to ask!" Becky was excited, too.

"I will," I promised. "I'll see you later in ballet."

"Okay," Becky agreed.

I hung up.

Bargain ballet, I thought. I liked the sound of that.

Later that morning I waited for Pat in the hallway outside Studio C. I wanted to ask her about bargain ballet lessons. But I didn't want Charlotte to hear.

"Hi, Katie," Pat said when she finally came down the hall. "What are you doing out here?"

"I want to ask you something," I explained. "Could I get a discount on my ballet lessons?"

"A discount? How come?" Pat asked.

"My parents are having another baby," I explained. "They can't afford to pay for my lessons anymore."

Pat looked thoughtful. "I don't think the school offers discounts on classes," she said. "At least, I've never heard about it. But I'll try to find a way to help you."

"Help me how?" I asked.

"I don't know," Pat said. "I'll have to talk to Madame Trikilnova."

"Thanks, Pat," I said, but my heart sank. I didn't think Pat could help me. Madame Trikilnova wouldn't do anything to keep me at her school. She thought I was a lazy troublemaker.

Sixteen

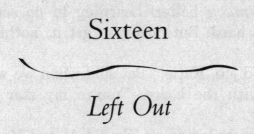

Left Out

"Hello, everybody!" Pat yelled as we walked into class.

Charlotte the Show-off had moved back to the front.

Megan was standing in her usual spot way in the back. She waved me over. "I saved you a place," she said.

"But if I stand here, Pat won't be able to see you," I teased Megan.

Megan grinned. "That's the idea. Isn't it great to have Pat back?"

"Yeah," I agreed. "Everyone looks happier."

"Even Al," Megan said.

I glanced over at Al. He usually plays scales to warm up. That day he was playing a jazzy song.

"Okay, guys," Pat said. "Let's get started."

I enjoyed all the barre that morning. Even the

ronds de jambe en l'air. My *ronds de jambe* were getting *much* better. Learning to do something right is hard. But once you get it, nothing feels better.

"Good job, Katie!" Pat said when we were finished with the barre. "You're my star student today."

Becky smiled at me. So did Al and Megan and almost everyone else. Madame Trikilnova had picked on me all during the last class. It sounded funny to hear nice things about my dancing. Pat's praise made me feel much better.

During the center work that afternoon, I stood up straighter than ever. I used my stomach muscles to help turn out my legs. Pat didn't praise me again, but I could feel how well I was dancing.

"We're going to spend the rest of class learning a partners dance," Pat announced when we finished our center work. "It's called the Grandfather's Dance and it's from the first act of *The Nutcracker*."

"Partners?" Becky whispered to me.

I nodded.

"I already know the Grandfather's Dance," Charlotte complained. Charlotte had been a party child in *The Nutcracker* the year before. She bragged about it all the time.

"Then I expect to see some fancy footwork from you," Pat told her.

Charlotte rolled her eyes.

Pat showed us how to line up. She taught us the steps of the dance. It was simple.

Becky wrinkled her nose. "The music is so slow."

"I guess that's why they call it the *Grandfather's* Dance," I said. "Grandfathers are slow, too."

The whole class did the dance together. We got to spin around in a lot of circles. It was fun.

I was surprised when Pat announced that class was over. Already? I thought.

We all clapped for Pat and Al. I felt sad. Only one more class to go.

Megan ran and got her dance bag from near the door.

"I got a letter from Jillian today," she announced. "There were even pictures!"

"Show us!" Becky demanded.

"I want to see the photographs, too," Pat added.

Becky, Nikki, Risa, Pat, and I huddled around Megan.

Megan pulled out the pictures and handed them to Pat.

Pat looked at the first one and passed it on.

One by one the pictures moved around the circle.

"This one is at the Lincoln Center," Pat said, holding up a snapshot. "That's the School of American Ballet in the background."

I studied the picture. In it Jillian and Heather had their arms around each other. Heather was dressed for class. She was grinning broadly.

"What does the letter say?" Becky asked.

"Read it," Megan told her.

Becky took the letter from Megan. "'Hi, everyone,'" she read. "'I'm having a great time in New York. Heather is staying with me at my dad's apartment.'"

"We already knew all that," I complained.

"Jillian didn't know we were going to talk to her mother," Megan pointed out.

"What else did Jillian write?" Risa asked.

"'Dad took us to see *Cats* on Broadway,'" Becky read.

"What's *Cats*?" Nikki asked.

"It's a play," Pat explained. "A musical. There's lots of dancing in it."

Nikki laughed. "I should have guessed that."

"I can't wait to study in New York," Becky said with that faraway look in her eyes.

"Me neither," Megan said.

"Do you guys really want to go to the School of American Ballet?" Pat asked.

Everyone nodded.

Everyone except me.

"Then you're going to have to work hard," Pat said.

"What's it like there?" Becky asked.

"I was there a long time ago," Pat said. "I'm sure lots of things have changed."

"Well, what was it like when you were there?" Becky insisted.

"Come on, Pat," Megan put in. "Tell us."

Pat started to answer my friends' questions. I let myself get pushed to the back of the circle. I didn't want to hear Pat's stories. I had only one more ballet class left. I would never study in New York.

I felt worse than ever.

Seventeen

Last Class

On Wednesday Dad, Alison, and I went to the library in Seattle. When the library closed, we picked up Mom at work. Then we went to dinner at my auntie Rose's house.

Auntie Rose is actually my dad's aunt. She's an old lady. Auntie Rose always makes spaghetti and tomato sauce when we come over. It's the only thing without meat she knows how to make.

I didn't see my friends all day. That was a relief. I didn't want them to remind me that my last ballet class was the next day.

Still, the next day came. It was suddenly afternoon. Becky was climbing up the stairs to my room.

"It's time for my last ballet class," I greeted her.

"Are you okay?" Becky asked me.

"I guess," I said.

112

We walked to the ballet school without saying much. I didn't feel like talking. We tramped up the ballet school steps, went inside, and pushed open the door of the dressing room.

"Hi, Katie!"

"Jillian!" I said. "I forgot you were coming back today. I can't believe you've been gone for only two weeks. It feels longer. Tons of stuff has happened."

"Megan told me you couldn't take classes anymore," Jillian said. "I'll miss you."

"Don't worry," I said. "Glory is a small town. You'll see me."

Megan came up and gave me a hug. She was crying.

Risa looked as if she was about to cry, too.

I knew how Risa felt. I sniffled.

"This stinks," Nikki said. "I'm not going to have anyone to be late with now."

"I'll teach you everything we learn in class," Becky promised.

"It won't be the same thing," I said.

"I know," Becky admitted. "But I'll teach you anyway."

"Thanks," I said.

We finished getting dressed. Then we dragged ourselves up to the studio.

"Katie, I'm glad you're here," Pat said.

"Madame Trikilnova wants to see you. She's in her office. Hurry down there and get back fast. I don't want you to miss the entire barre."

I gave my friends a surprised look.

Megan shrugged.

Risa and Nikki and Jillian looked confused.

"Go on," Becky told me.

"What does Madame Trikilnova want?" I asked Pat.

"Go downstairs and find out," Pat suggested.

I opened the door and let myself out of the studio. But I didn't go to Madame Trikilnova's office. Instead I stood in the hall, right next to the door of Studio C. I didn't want to see Madame Trikilnova. I was sure she was going to yell at me about something. *What did I do wrong?* I wondered.

The sound of the piano drifted out into the hall. I was wondering how long I should wait before going back into the studio, when Becky came out.

"Hi," I said, embarrassed.

"I *knew* you would still be out here." Becky took my hand. "Come on. You have to see what Madame Trikilnova wants."

"How come?" I asked.

"Maybe it'll be something good," Becky said.

I dragged my feet. "Maybe it'll be something bad."

"Why do you think that?" Becky asked.

"Because Madame Trikilnova hates me," I said.

Becky got behind me and pushed me toward the stairs. "Madame Trikilnova does not hate you," she said. "Now, stop being such a chicken."

I hate to be called a chicken. Becky knows that, and she was using it against me. Still, I let her hurry me down the stairs.

Becky stood and watched until I knocked on Madame Trikilnova's office door. Then she ran back to class.

"Come in!" Madame Trikilnova yelled.

I pushed the door open.

"Yes, Miss Ruiz?" Madame Trikilnova greeted me. She was sitting at her desk, reading a piece of paper. Her glasses were perched on the tip of her nose.

"Pat said you wanted to see me," I explained. I was still hoping that Pat had made a mistake.

But Madame Trikilnova nodded. "Yes, I did," she said. "Pat told me you wanted a discount on your lessons."

"Yes," I said. "A *big* discount."

Madame Trikilnova raised her eyebrows.

Quickly I explained about my mother being pregnant. "I guess babies are pretty expensive," I finished.

"They are," Madame Trikilnova agreed. "Miss Ruiz, I want to ask you a question. Have you ever worked very hard?"

I thought for a second, then nodded. "My friends and I tried to earn the money for my lessons. We started an odd-jobs business. One day we did five jobs."

"Do you like working?" Madame Trikilnova asked.

"Sure," I said.

"Why?"

That was a silly question. "Because I like getting paid," I said with a shrug.

"I see." Madame Trikilnova studied my face. "I don't think ballet is important to you. You don't work hard in class."

"You're wrong!" I blurted out. "I love ballet."

"Then why don't you work harder?" Madame Trikilnova asked.

"Well, I didn't always *know* I loved it," I admitted. "I didn't know until I found out I couldn't take class anymore."

Madame Trikilnova nodded. "I want to offer you a deal. You can help me around the office here. In exchange I will give you a discount on the price of your classes."

I could hardly believe my ears. "I—I have to

116

ask my parents," I said. "But I'm sure they'll say yes. And it sounds great to me!"

"I'll call your parents and work out the details," Madame Trikilnova said. "But before you accept, I want you to understand this is not a gift. You must work every weekday morning for the rest of the summer. After school starts you will come in Saturday mornings. You will have to answer the phone, run errands—do whatever I ask you."

"That's fine," I said eagerly. "I'll work really, really hard. You'll see."

"Then we have a deal," Madame Trikilnova said. "If your parents agree, you can begin tomorrow morning at nine. And don't be late."

"Okay," I said. "Thanks!"

"That is all," Madame Trikilnova said. "Go back to your class now."

I jumped up. I ran upstairs, feeling terrific. But by the time I got to the second floor, something was bothering me. Why was Madame Trikilnova being so nice? I didn't understand.

Eighteen

Back to Class

"Hurry and warm up," Pat told me back in class. "You've already missed most of the barre."

I hurried to my usual place.

Becky gave me a questioning look as I passed her. I grinned at her.

"Take your time," Nikki whispered to me. "I think *ronds de jambe en l'air* are going to be next."

"But those are my favorite," I whispered back.

I turned my back to Nikki. I put my left hand on the barre and eased into a *demi-plié*. I was facing Risa.

"What did Madame Trikilnova want?" Risa whispered.

I didn't answer.

"Did she yell?" Risa whispered.

I did a *relevé* and turned. Now I was facing Nikki.

"You look happy!" she whispered.

I *was* happy—so happy I was practically bursting.

"I'll tell you later," I told Nikki and Risa. I didn't want to interrupt the class by whispering. Besides, I had to think about my stretches. I wanted to be warmed up in time for the *ronds de jambe*.

I was.

Pat walked down the center of the studio. She stopped in front of each of us and studied our dancing.

"Nice work," Pat said when she got to me. "Your turnout looks good today."

I grinned at her. *I'm going to be taking classes in the fall,* I reminded myself. I felt incredibly lucky.

"Take a two-minute break," Pat told us when we finished the barre. "But no more than two minutes! We have to start the center work before your muscles get cold." (I think Pat gave us a break only because she knew I had big news.)

All my friends ran over to me.

"What's up?" Nikki demanded.

"I can't believe it," Becky said. "But I think I was right. Madame Trikilnova *did* want something good."

119

"I get to stay!" I hollered. I told my friends about my deal with Madame Trikilnova as quickly as I could. Pat listened, too.

"That's incredible!"

"Fantastic!"

"I'm happy I didn't lose you," Pat told me.

I threw my arms around Pat's neck. "You did this," I said. "You talked Madame Trikilnova into helping me. Thank you so much!"

Pat hugged me back. "You're welcome."

Charlotte sighed. "Can we get back to work?"

"Good idea," I said.

When class started up again, I concentrated as I had never concentrated before. I took class more seriously than I ever had. Now that I knew how important ballet was to me, I planned to make every minute in every class count.

Nineteen

A Girl's Name

On Friday morning I woke up at 8:20. I got dressed and ate breakfast quickly.

"Where are you going?" Alison asked as I headed for the door. She was sitting at the kitchen table in her pajamas, eating a bowl of cereal.

"To work!" I announced. I ran out the door and toward the ballet school. When I got there, everything was locked up tight. I sat down on the steps to wait. Madame Trikilnova arrived as the town clock started to strike nine o'clock.

"Good morning, Miss Ruiz," she said.

"Good morning," I replied.

Madame Trikilnova unlocked the ballet school's heavy front door.

I tried to act calm. But my heart was beating a million miles a minute. I was nervous about spending the morning in a tiny office with Madame Trikilnova.

"The first thing I want you to do every morning is make coffee," Madame Trikilnova told me. "Do you know how?"

"I know how to make instant," I said.

Madame Trikilnova wrinkled her nose. "I don't like instant coffee," she announced. "We'll make the real stuff."

She opened a little closet and showed me where the coffee filters were. She showed me how to measure out the right amount of coffee, pour in the right amount of water, and turn on the machine.

Next Madame Trikilnova opened the tiny refrigerator under the window. "We're out of milk," she reported. "I will give you some money. You can go buy some more."

"Right," I agreed. I took the money Madame Trikilnova offered me, ran all the way to the store, bought the milk, and ran back.

I was gone about five minutes. When I walked back into the office, Madame Trikilnova handed me a list. "This should keep you busy for a while," she said.

Madame Trikilnova sat down at her desk and started to study some papers. She didn't say anything more.

I glanced down at the list and got to work.

I watered the plants in the office.

I fed Giselle. She purred when I petted her head. I was happy she'd forgiven me for stepping on her paw.

I straightened up the table in the front hall. Then I quietly let myself into the office.

Madame Trikilnova looked up at me.

"I finished everything on the list," I told her.

Madame Trikilnova got up. She showed me a stack of the ballet school's flyers, which were just like the one Sophie had shown me at the Hills'. She asked me to fold each one in thirds and tape it shut. I had just started when the phone rang.

"Hello?" Madame Trikilnova said. "Maurice! How are you?"

Madame Trikilnova sounded delighted. She sat down on top of her desk and started to chat with Maurice. It seemed like he was a good friend of hers.

I was shocked. Madame Trikilnova had a friend! A friend named *Maurice*. Maybe he was her boyfriend. Hmm. Working at the ballet school was going to be very interesting. I relaxed a little.

Madame Trikilnova hung up the phone.

I was feeling pretty brave. "Madame Trikilnova," I said. "Why did you give me this job?"

123

"What do you mean 'why'?" Madame Trikilnova demanded. She was back to her old grumpy self. "Why shouldn't I offer you a job?"

"I—I just didn't think you liked me very much," I blurted out.

Madame Trikilnova didn't seem surprised. "I think I understand," she said after considering for a minute. "Because I correct you in class, you think I don't like you. Is that it?"

"Yes," I admitted.

"But that is not so," Madame Trikilnova said. "I only correct you because I want you to work harder. You must work harder—much harder! You have talent. It must not go to waste."

Madame Trikilnova picked on me because she thought I was a good dancer. That was a shock. I thought it was because I was *bad*. I felt proud.

"I'll do my very best in class from now on," I promised her.

"Pat told me you have already changed," Madame Trikilnova said to me. "She says you are thinking about what you're doing."

"Really?" I asked with a big grin.

Madame Trikilnova looked a little uneasy. "Yes," she said, getting to her feet. "Now I must go to lunch."

Once Madame Trikilnova was gone, I snooped

around the office. I found a secret stash of pepper-mints in her top desk drawer.

I examined a yellowed certificate hanging in a frame behind Madame Trikilnova's desk. It was written in a strange language. I had no idea what the certificate said. But I could make out the word "Vaganova." That was the famous ballet school in Russia where Madame Trikilnova trained.

Madame Trikilnova's full name was written on the certificate in old-fashioned handwriting. Her name was Stacia Ana Trikilnova. Stacia. What a great name!

Twenty

Tiny Tennis Shoes

"Thank you, Miss Ruiz," Madame Trikilnova told me. She had just gotten back from lunch. "You were a big help this morning. You may go now. Miss Hill and your other friends are waiting for you outside."

I jumped out of my chair. "I'll see you on Monday," I said. "Have a great weekend."

Madame Trikilnova actually smiled at me! "I hope you enjoy your weekend, too," she told me.

"I will!" I told her.

I hurried outside.

Becky, Jillian, Megan, Risa, and Nikki were sitting on the ballet school steps.

"How was it?" Megan asked as soon as she saw me.

"Great!" I said, plopping down next to her.

Nikki's eyes grew wide. "Madame Trikilnova

127

didn't yell at you the whole time or anything?" she asked.

I laughed. "Nope. It was fine."

"Did you tell your parents about your job?" Becky asked.

"Sure," I said.

"And they don't mind?" Becky asked.

"No," I replied. "I told them how important ballet was to me. They're happy I found a way to keep taking lessons."

"So are we," Megan said.

I smiled. "My parents think I'll learn a lot of responsibility from having a job," I said. "When school starts, I'm only allowed to work a few hours each week. Mom says I have to have enough time to study."

"Madame Trikilnova said that was okay?" Jillian asked.

I nodded.

"This looks like the end of our odd-jobs business," Risa said.

"I want to talk to you guys about that," I said. "I still have the twenty-two dollars we earned together. I don't need the money anymore. I think we should split it."

"Great!" Nikki said.

"Let's divide it evenly," Megan suggested. "There

are six of us. What's twenty-two divided by six?"

"Wait," Jillian said with a laugh. "I shouldn't get any money. I was in New York when you guys earned it."

"Oh, right," Megan said. "That means I need to divide by five. Does anyone have a piece of paper and a pencil?"

"Hold on," Risa said. "I only helped for one day. I don't deserve as much money as Megan and Katie and Becky."

"Me either," Nikki agreed. "I was shopping while you guys worked."

"We didn't earn anything the second day," I pointed out.

"But the three of you worked more hours," Nikki said.

"I have an idea," Becky said. "We could spend the money together. That way we wouldn't have to figure out how much belongs to each of us."

"Good idea," I said.

Everyone else agreed.

"So what should we buy?" Risa asked.

"Training bras," Nikki suggested.

Everyone laughed. None of us had anything to put in a bra.

"We could go see the Pacific Northwest Ballet," Becky suggested.

"We don't have enough money for that," I said. "Ballet tickets are expensive."

"Let's buy something for Katie's new little brother or sister," Megan suggested.

I was happy when everyone agreed to that.

"What should we get?" Jillian asked.

"What does the baby need?" Risa asked.

"Almost everything," I said. "My parents weren't planning to have any more children. They gave away all the stuff Alison and I used."

Becky jumped up. "Let's shop!" she suggested.

Only one store in Glory sells baby stuff: Tyler's Boutique. That's where we headed.

Tyler's Boutique is a fancy store just off Main Street. I try to avoid the place. Once, when I was little, I touched a bird feeder in Tyler's. It fell and broke. Mrs. Tyler made my mother pay for it. I've gone into Tyler's with my mother a few times since then. Mom always says "don't touch" over and over. It makes me jumpy.

"May I help you?" Mrs. Tyler asked when we walked in.

"We're looking for a baby present," Jillian said.

Mrs. Tyler smiled sweetly. (Sometimes being the new kid in town is great. Jillian had never broken anything in Tyler's.)

"I have some lovely frocks," Mrs. Tyler said.

She headed to the back of the store.

Jillian followed Mrs. Tyler.

We all followed Jillian.

"What's a frock?" Nikki whispered.

"How should I know?" I replied.

Mrs. Tyler showed Jillian some fancy baby clothes made out of velvet and lace. We all peeked over Jillian's shoulder.

"Now I understand," Nikki whispered. "A frock is a dress a kid could ruin in five minutes."

"These are lovely," Jillian told Mrs. Tyler. "But we can only afford to spend twenty-two dollars."

"I see," Mrs. Tyler said. She led us over to a counter. She pointed out the things we had enough money to buy.

We finally agreed to get a pair of tiny tennis shoes. They were super cute. Jillian asked Mrs. Tyler to wrap up the shoes. Mrs. Tyler did it for free.

The shoes cost $15.28. I paid for them and got out of Tyler's as fast as possible. Becky, Risa, Megan, and Nikki were right behind me. Jillian followed more slowly.

Back on the sidewalk, I took a deep breath.

"That was fun," Jillian said. "I love to shop."

I didn't answer her. Instead I counted the money in my pocket. "We still have $6.72 left," I reported. "Why don't we get some milk shakes?"

"Let's go!" Risa said.

A few minutes later we were sitting at our favorite booth in the coffee shop. Our glasses were already half-empty.

"There's your mother, and Alison," Nikki told me.

Alison had spotted us, too. She dragged Mom into the coffee shop.

"Hi!" Alison shouted. "I found the absolutely bestest boy's name in the whole world."

"That's great," Risa said. "What is it?"

"The name is . . ." Alison didn't tell us right away. She has a good sense of drama. "Fred!"

"Like Fred the dinosaur on TV?" I asked.

Alison nodded proudly.

Everyone burst out laughing.

Mom gave us a merry look.

Alison had reminded me of something. "I thought of a girl's name I like," I announced. "It's Stacia."

"That's a great name," Becky said.

"It's really pretty."

"Cool."

"How did you think of it?" Megan asked.

I smiled. "It just came to me."

"Come on, Alison," Mom said, pulling on her hand. "We need to get going."

"I want to stay with Katie," Alison said.

"No," Mom said.

"Please," Alison said.

"It's okay, Mom. I don't mind if she stays."

"Are you sure?" Mom asked.

"Absolutely," I told her.

"Okay," Mom said. "See you kids later."

Alison was beaming. She pulled a chair up to the booth.

"Do you want an ice-cream cone?" I asked Alison.

She nodded.

"You're going to buy it with your own money?" Risa asked.

"Sure," I said.

"You're a great big sister," Becky told me.

"It isn't always easy," I said.

Alison's eyes grew big. "Being a big sister is hard?" she asked, sounding worried.

"Sometimes," I admitted. "But it's also the best job in the whole wide world."

Grand Jeté

The Five Basic Positions

First position

Second position

Third position

Fourth position

Fifth position

WHAT THE BALLET WORDS MEAN

Dégagé (day-ga-ZHAY) An exercise in which you stretch your foot out, lift your toe off the ground, put your toe down, and then bring your foot back in. You can do it to the front, side, or back.

Demi-plié (de-MEE plee-AY) A half knee-bend.

Développés (dayv-law-PAY) An exercise in which the dancer slowly stretches out her leg.

En bas (ahn bah) A low position of the arms.

Grand (gron) means "big" or "large" in French. A *grand plié* is bigger than a *plié*.

Jeté (je-TAY) A type of jump. In a *grand jeté* the dancer opens her arms and legs wide.

Pirouette (peer-oo-ET) is French for "whirl." It's a kind of turn in which the dancer spins around on one foot.

Plié (plee-AY) is a knee bend. A *grand plié* is bigger than a *plié*.

Positions Almost every step in ballet begins and ends with the dancer's feet in one of five positions. The positions are called first, second, third, fourth, and fifth. The drawing on p. 135 shows how the positions look. Some ballet instructors use French words to describe the positions: *première, seconde, troisième, quatrième,* and *cinquième*.

Relevé (ruhluh-VAY) An exercise in which you rise up on the balls of your feet.

Rond de jambe à terre (rawn duh zhamb a tehr) is

a movement in which the leg draws a half circle on the ground.

Rond de jambe en l'air (rawn duh zhamb ahn lehr) is a movement in which the leg draws a circle in the air.

Tendu (tahn-DEW) An exercise in which you stretch one foot along the floor without bending your knees. Also called *battement tendu*.